The Grimm Cases

Origins

By: Lyla Oweds

Cover Design by

Crimson Phoenix Creations

Edited by

EAL Editing Services, Jessica Westover, Tara Mcnabb and Mary Swedo

Second edition edited by

Heather Long and Becky Stewart

Special Thanks to

My TAFF Family and Matthew for inspiration and encouragement

Table of Contents

Chapter One

Haunted

"The place I'm house sitting is haunted."

My statement was brave—considering—and I hoped I'd spoken loud enough to be heard by the intended recipient. I didn't want to repeat myself. It had taken a lot of courage—or foolhardiness—to say it the first time.

The paranormal was one of those difficult-to-approach topics, especially with my best friend. History had proven our differences of opinion. Despite being inseparable for over ten years, I knew this was a topic where we were unlikely to reach a consensus.

But at this point, I was desperate. I might be going crazy, and only Finn could help me.

Yet, there was no response. No reaction.

Across the small cafe table, Finn furiously typed on his laptop—undisturbed by my nervous confession. He'd made no outward acknowledgment of my words, and it made me wonder if he'd even heard me.

The coffee shop was rather loud, after all.

"Finn." I pressed my foot against his shin, trying to get his attention. "Finn, did you hear what I just told you?"

With perfect lips turned downward, he glanced up, meeting my gaze. His gray eyes were normally playful and light, but at the moment were sharp—disapproving. At once, I was thankful his black-rimmed glasses offered a filter for his judgment.

"I heard you." His distinctive baritone dipped an octave lower than normal, signaling his annoyance. "Considering the absurdity of what you said, I chose to ignore it."

Then without further ado, he refocused his attention on his laptop.

I gasped. How could he be so callous and uncaring?

Even if he didn't believe me, he could at least hear me out. He was my best friend and the only person in the world I cared about besides my parents. But he could be such a jerk!

I was being *haunted*. I could *die*.

"Finn, what if I'm not wrong?" I asked, desperate. I needed him to take me seriously. Just this once. I was opening a can of worms, but I didn't know what else to do at this point. "Wouldn't you feel terrible if I were killed by an angry poltergeist and you could have done something to stop it?"

"I *would* feel bad if you were killed by an angry ghost." Finn pushed his glasses up his nose, dragging his gaze to mine. "However, I have nothing to be worried about. *If* ghosts and demons even existed, then it certainly wouldn't be a harmless poltergeist that ended up killing you. Not with the kind of trouble that you tend to attract. You need to learn to relax."

My heart fell and my pulse began to race. *Trouble*. I never got into any kind of trouble. In fact, I was the opposite of a troublemaker. Finn was being incredibly rude. Some best friend.

I glared at my untouched coffee while Finn returned to his homework—or whatever he seemed intent on.

Adrenaline was rushing through me, an expected reaction to the mental build-up I'd gone through to approach this topic. With Finn so quick to shoot me down, there was nothing left for me to talk about. There was no way for me to relax, to concentrate on my own assignments.

I had risked a lot by bringing this up.

Finn and I were as different as could be. He was a hot nerd in all the ways hot nerds can be, including researching the most efficient way to maximize the results of his daily exercise routine. Meanwhile, I preferred to sleep in and avoid sweating at all costs. He was blunt and not shy.

Definitely not like me.

Sometimes I wondered how it was possible for people with contrasting personalities to be so close. Now that we lived on campus, our contrasts were more obvious than ever. He was adjusting to college life well, but me...

I was constantly on the edge of my seat. Besides my roommate, who kept to herself, Finn was the only person on campus I was comfortable around. If it hadn't been for our nightly study sessions, I wasn't sure how I'd cope.

Seeing him always made me feel better.

It wasn't just because I'd crushed on him since childhood. There was something about being *with* him that managed to put me at ease. I admired him. I always had. And throughout all of our years of friendship, he'd taken care of me.

For ten years, he never complained about my quirks, and I loved him for it. It was for *him* that I was trying to step outside of my comfort zone, to earn money and test my limits by house sitting for my biology professor. If he saw I was trying to grow as a person, maybe he'd finally ask me to be his girlfriend. When Professor Hamway asked me to take care of her conservatory while she visited her daughter, I'd agreed.

Finn had no idea *why* I wanted to house sit for her. However, he hadn't objected. He probably assumed I was doing this for access to her nursery, which I adored.

He wouldn't be entirely wrong.

But there was something not so great about this job—the ghost that was trying to kill me.

"Finn." I had no choice. I *had* to convince him. If I didn't, I was going to die. He'd believed me once, so maybe he would again. "Listen to me." I needed to convey the seriousness of this situation to him. My mind raced, searching for the words. "When I woke up last night, and I wasn't able to move or talk. I think the spirit was trying to suffocate me. That wasn't in my head!"

He didn't say anything as he hovered his hands in place over his keyboard. Instead, he frowned.

That pause gave me hope.

"Please believe me," I begged. He was my best friend, he had to—

Finn sighed and closed his laptop. He then removed his glasses and pinched the bridge of his nose—a clear sign he was annoyed. "Bianca, what do you expect me to do? I'm not a doctor. I've told you that sleep paralysis is normal."

"Take me seriously. Please just hear me out." I was close to tears now. I had been sure that he would listen to logic. How could he not care? I was terrified to go back to that house, but I had no choice. I had made a commitment, and I always kept my promises.

And I really needed the money.

I didn't expect him to fix my problem. I just needed his *permission*. It would be rude to introduce myself. I needed him to make the introductions.

My plan, after all, involved his brother.

"Didn't you say Damen is into the supernatural? Doesn't he teach here too? If he's nearby, maybe he could help. He might have some ideas. If you could just talk to him and—"

"You don't need to talk to Damen," Finn snapped before he opened his eyes. He reached for my hand. "And I *am* taking you seriously."

His touch was a balm to my fear. Despite being scared—and annoyed—I

8

couldn't keep from being distracted. For a moment, my attention strayed and my heart beat so quickly that it felt as though it would fly right out of my chest.

In those moments, nothing existed outside of the two of us. His mouth quirked and his eyes softened. In these moments, I suspected that Finn had feelings for me too. Especially based on comments he'd made in the past. Insinuations that I belonged to him.

Being near him made me feel funny inside, but it was hard to trust myself. And we'd known each other for so long I couldn't contemplate my life without him. I wanted to be with him forever. I had it all planned out.

But then he spoke, and the warm feeling vanished. "Have you been taking your medication? You know what happens when you forget."

Terrifying shadows swam along my peripheral vision. The suffocating sensations. Feeling as though I perpetually hovered on the edge of a cliff. The sense of being hunted, never safe.

I had to work through all of this myself. I had to get better. Despite what Finn believed, I had to learn to survive on my own. Besides, my anxieties never seemed to subside with medication. Pharmaceutical intervention was clearly ineffective. I guess I would just have to chalk this up as a difference of opinion and move on.

Finn knew this about me. I told him many years ago. But I'd learned better than to talk about my symptoms.

Yet, I had thought if I just had proof…something outside of my personal senses—physical proof of a haunting. Then maybe he'd understand.

This wasn't fair. All he had to do was *show up* at my professor's home. Just once. Then he'd be able to see it for himself!

But it didn't seem like that would ever happen. Instead of listening to a word I said, he began to talk about my medication. If I insisted on discussing the haunting after his initial rejection, he'd worry. And if that happened, he'd tell my parents and they would get involved.

It was unfair—but at the same time, he was trying in his own way. After all, Finn looked out for me. He cared. He tried to work with the weirdness of my life.

He just didn't understand...

Regardless, it wasn't right he'd brushed off my concerns and didn't take me seriously. Good intentions or not.

It became harder to breathe, and my chest felt heavy. It wasn't often that I became genuinely angry with Finn, but the topic of my medication was always a sensitive one. "Why do you do that?"

Why did he have to ruin everything?

"Bianca." He watched me with renewed wariness, suspicion lacing his gray eyes. "You didn't answer my question."

"I'm doing what I should," I replied, holding back tears so he wouldn't know how much he was hurting me. He didn't care about my concerns, or the haunting. Right away, he assumed that it was my paranoia speaking. Why couldn't he trust me, just this once? "Your question is irrelevant." I needed to leave. I'd rather face the angry spirit than deal with being patronized this way.

I gathered my notebooks and began to shove them into my backpack, no longer able to look at him. "I'll go bother someone who wants to hear what I have to say."

As I turned to leave, Finn's voice stopped me. "Who are you going to talk to, Bianca? You don't talk to people."

My breath caught, and I couldn't stop myself from glancing back at him. He hadn't moved from his seat. The expression on his face that betrayed his thoughts: I was crazy.

His dusty blond hair fell over his forehead. And he looked so sincere at the moment I wanted to apologize—to not be angry. He only cared. I had no reason to be upset.

But I was.

All he'd had to do was listen to me, and he'd refused. If I told him any more, he'd change from concerned to domineering in an instant. I couldn't afford for that to happen.

"Sorry to bother you." I took a step back, which seemed to startle him. "I've been tired lately. I'll talk to you later."

"Bianca?"

"Bye."

And for the first time in my life, I walked away from Finn Abernathy.

Huddling under my covers, I tried to ignore the presence in the room. Surely it could only possibly be an evil spirit with the intention of sucking out my soul. But it wasn't making a move yet, so there was nothing I could do about it right now.

Currently, my greatest concern was Finn's anger with me. I walked away earlier, not thinking things through. But what if I lost my only friend over this?

Without anyone who cared, I might as well let the ghost drag me into the flames of eternal hell. I would welcome the journey. Perhaps a demon or two might want to be friends.

But even more frightening—what if Finn decided to snoop around behind my back? What if he checked my prescription?

I shouldn't have brushed him off.

It was one o'clock in the morning, according to the chimes of the grandfather clock in the hallway. Maybe he would still be awake. Would he mind if I sent him a message?

I couldn't stay angry with him. He had to know this.

I snatched the phone from the bedside table and pulled up my contacts. I easily located Finn, considering that there were only four numbers in my contacts: my parents' landline, their cells, and Finn's cell.

I wasn't sure how to approach my apology. The best bet would be to pretend nothing had happened. It was the most foolproof way to escape this conflict.

Me: *Are you asleep already? I didn't get a chance to say goodnight.*

I hit send before second guessing myself. While I had been the first to cave, it would essentially be up to him to ans—

My phone chirped and I blinked at it stupidly for a moment. Never before had he responded so quickly. I had been expecting him to wait until later in the morning, at least.

Maybe this was worse than I thought. He might actually be calling it quits and messaging me to tell me so.

My hands shook as I pulled open the message, too curious to procrastinate. I looked across the room toward where I knew the evil spirit to be, a chill sliding down my spine. *Five more minutes, then you can take me to your master.*

The heavy feeling in the room increased substantially, as if the ghost heard my mental promise.

But it seemed as though my fears had been for naught. At least about Finn.

Finn: *What are you still doing awake? Are you feeling better now? I was worried.*

Did this mean he wasn't angry with me? It was almost too much to consider. Then again, Finn avoided confrontation. That was one thing we did have in common.

But how should I respond? I wanted to be honest, but I simply couldn't. There was no way I could admit that I was certain there was a ghost sitting across from me, touching my foot over the top of the covers. No way could I admit to him that I felt as if I was living in a nightmare. It would only start another argument.

I couldn't even ask him to stop by, just to keep me company. It would look suspicious, considering our earlier conversation.

No, I couldn't discuss this with him ever again. He had made that abundantly clear.

Me: *Everything is perfect. I'll meet you tomorrow at our usual place.*

Somehow, I ended up here—in the liberal arts building, within the maze doubling as the psychology faculty's hallways. It was bright and early on Saturday morning. I was lucky that a staff meeting had taken place earlier so the building was open. True to the secretary's directions, I had discovered Dr. Gregory Stephens's office.

Hopefully, Damen would be here.

Now I needed to muster up enough courage to enact the next stage of my plan.

I certainly hadn't intended to stalk Damen Abernathy's mentor when I fell asleep last night. But when I woke and discovered the dishes in the kitchen had been stacked neatly by some unknown being during the night, I just had to do this. If *that* wasn't an actual physical sign of a haunting, I didn't know what was.

Clearly, Finn would be no help. I had no other choice but to take matters into my own hands.

Even so, this probably wasn't my most brilliant plan. I had never even met Damen before. Finn only ever complained about his estranged brother. They rarely interacted—each parent deciding to raise their boys separately outside of holidays.

All I knew about Damen was his interest in the paranormal—something Finn was cynical about—and that Damen was a few years older than the two of us. Damen, to my understanding, had graduated college early and was back at his alma mater. He had an internship in forensic psychology and worked with the local police when he wasn't student teaching.

I braced myself, unable to move toward the door. Even if he did have an interest, would he believe me? I could be opening myself up to a whole new level of ridicule by talking to him.

And the talking…This would be difficult. I had no idea how to interact with people. But I supposed I needed to get over it. Damen was *practically* family—or he would be, once Finn and I became official and finally got married. Plus, if I wanted to get technical, he was *kind of* a professor. And they weren't so bad.

Of course, if Finn ever found out I had come here…

Well, he would be livid. But that was *if* Finn ever found out. If Damen and Finn didn't interact, then maybe Damen helping me with a haunting would never come up. I would take my chances—I'd do anything to not be haunted.

But first, I needed to work up the courage to knock on the professor's door.

My heart pounded as my mind mentally screamed encouragements. Nothing bad would happen; professors were good people. Besides, I was already growing as a person, just by stepping outside of my comfort zone. I could do this. *Just, please Lord, please don't let him be ugly.*

I caught myself, wondering why the absurd thought even crossed my mind. Him being ugly would only *help* this confrontation. If only slightly.

After wiping my sweaty palm on my thigh, I raised my hand to knock. I could do this. With a deep breath, I moved my closed fist toward the door, only to freeze.

Please don't laugh at me.

Closing my eyes, I raised my hand again. *Come on, Bianca. Knock.*

My eyes flew open. What if he wasn't here? What if I'd done this all for nothing?

My heart thundered, feeling as if it would pound out of my chest.

Actually, it was unlikely he was here, come to think of it. There was a staff meeting, but Damen was kind of a staff member. And the noise that I heard coming from the office could be audio feedback. He was probably back home since it was a Saturday.

I'd come back another day.

I spun around to leave and hadn't made it three steps before the door opened behind me.

"Who the devil are you?" a sharp voice demanded. Abrupt and unfriendly, it stopped me in my tracks. It was just my luck that Damen was meaner than I'd expected—and older.

"Turn around, girl, and talk to me," the voice demanded. "I haven't got all day. I'm not allowing any new transfers into my classes, if that's what you've come about."

My mind screamed at me to run away, but my body obeyed the man's stern command. It was too late to hide now. He had seen me and the secretary had my name. There was no escape.

"Mr...Abernathy?"

The tall, elderly man narrowed his eyes as he touched his wire-rimmed glasses with a manicured finger. "Damen Abernathy is not here; this is *my* office. What do you need? I have a consult to attend, so make it snappy."

This must be Dr. Stephens, then. But weren't professors supposed to be kindly?

"I'm sorry to interrupt..." I pulled at my sleeve as I focused on his brown loafers. "I need to talk to Damen Abernathy for a minute, if that's at all possible. My name is Bianca Brosnan, and I'm friends with Finn. The secretary told me…"

"*Finn?*" Dr. Stephens interrupted me, his voice curious.

I glanced up. He appeared to be deep in thought.

"Are we talking about the 'Finn' who happens to be Damen's shithead little brother?"

I frowned.

That seemed to be enough of a response for Dr. Stephens, and he continued. "I didn't know he had any friends. Who the hell would be stupid enough to put up with *him?*"

I wasn't even sure how to respond. I didn't generally argue with authority, but that wasn't very nice.

"You must not be…" He narrowed his eyes, studying me. "Why are you here, again?"

He forgot already? Perhaps he was senile—he did seem extremely old. "I need to talk to Damen. Do you know where he is?"

Dr. Stephens waved his hand in the air impatiently. "Yes, I got that much already. But *why* are you looking for him?"

I blinked at him—he was very nosy. Perhaps, since he was Damen's mentor, he was interested in the paranormal too? Maybe he'd understand and might be able to help?

"Because if you are here to ask him on a date, I'll have you know that he has no time for games." Dr. Stephens scrutinized me appraisingly. "You are a very attractive young lady. But before you have your heart broken by the follies of youth, I need to warn you that…"

"I'm not here to ask him on a date!" I blurted out, horrified that he would think such a thing. My cheeks burned with embarrassment, and I stared at a point over his shoulder to avoid looking at him.

"Then what is it, girl? Hurry it along." He crossed his arms impatiently. "Out with it. Clearly something is upsetting you."

"I'm being haunted!" My skyrocketing anxiety had me blurting out everything in a rush. "I mean, again. I've always been able to see things, but now it's getting worse. No one believes me. I tried to tell Finn…He said that his brother did ghost hunting stuff, so I thought that I could…"

My words slowed as the reality of what I had just done slammed into me. I hadn't been thinking, as usual. The fear at what was happening to me had temporarily overshadowed an even darker fear. And the expression on the professor's face was less than comforting.

He was staring at me as if I'd grown another head.

My heart raced as I screamed internally at having told a professor—a *psychology* professor—my absurd problems.

I had to make this better before I ended up locked in an asylum.

"April Fool's." I tried to laugh as I waved my hand in the air playfully.

I had to get out of there. I began to step back, and his expression changed from shock to acute amusement.

"It's September," he deadpanned.

I nervously laughed as I continued to inch backward, ready to make a run for it. He had to think it was a joke. Hopefully, I would never have a class with him. "Let's just forget that I was here, all right? Sorry to bother you."

"Wait," he commanded, and I froze. His face was carefully neutral. "Don't move." He turned around and walked back into his office.

I was in agony. I wanted to run, but he was a teacher. He said not to move. He could track me down.

And now, because of my big mouth, I was going to be institutionalized.

But if he had called the police, he'd done it quickly, because seconds later he was back.

"Here." He handed me a folded piece of paper. "Damen is gone today. But he has a meeting tonight for an outside association of which he is a member. There's only a few in the group, but I'm certain that they'd be interested in hearing your story."

I glanced at the paper which had a single address scrawled on it. As if that wasn't creepy. "Do I just—"

"It starts at six," Dr. Stephens cut me off. "Don't be late. Now, I'm sorry to rush you, but I really must be going." He pulled on a dark trench coat before nodding as he passed me in the hallway. "Don't get into trouble today, and we'll hope to see you there."

I glanced back at the paper, stunned, then looked up at his retreating form.

What did he mean, *we?*

Chapter Two

Strange

If anything was inconvenient about small towns, the lack of public transportation would rank high on the list. Of course, after looking up the address on my map app, I knew I'd have to step outside of my comfort zone…again. The university shuttle only went so far, and then I would have to walk a mile and a half to make the meeting. Which was fine. I'd never been a fan of some random picking me up in his car, service or not. I could walk.

I was going to have to walk in the middle of nowhere, in the mountains, when the evenings were getting colder. This was going to suck.

I should have mentioned to Dr. Stephens that I didn't have my license. Most of the students had a car, even if they were required to park off campus. However, my parents and Finn never wanted me to learn to drive because of my anxiety. As he repeatedly reminded me, it was safer that way. Normally, Finn was the one who drove me anywhere I needed to go.

But now I was on my own and had no choice. It wasn't as if I could ask Finn to drive me to meet his brother at a weird address for a cult meeting. He'd never agree, and it would ruin my plan of secrecy.

No, I had to go alone. It was risky. But if I perished, then it was for a greater cause.

All this angst for a meeting.

Perhaps it was a sign. Perhaps I shouldn't go. Hadn't the metallic banging noise stopped a short while ago? Surely, that was a good thing. Maybe the ghost had given up and moved on?

Probably not. Just two hours before, I had face-planted into the corner of a table when a stool was jerked out from under me. That had kind of sucked.

I tried to conceal my bruise as best as I could for the meeting and attempted to dress for both warmth and to impress. I generally didn't wear pants unless gardening. But with the sage green sweater, my jeans looked passable. After all, I did want to make a good impression on my potential, future brother-in-law.

Outwardly, I appeared somewhat decent. But inside, I was a mess. Being brave was quickly becoming old, and I hoped the rest of the evening wouldn't be too stressful. Otherwise, I had no idea how I'd hold it together.

One of the best ways to discourage small talk was to keep your nose buried in your phone. This skill also had the added benefit of allowing the user ample time to research. And I did like to be prepared for anything.

I unashamedly burned through my network's data usage as I searched the internet for various phrases such as: 'Do college professors need to have thorough background checks?' and 'What should you do if you suspect that you might be used in a cannibalistic ritual?'.

A young girl couldn't be too cautious. And despite the fact that a—supposedly—reputable professor invited me, planning for the worst-case-scenario was the best thing to do. Always.

Besides, what kind of well-intentioned professor writes down a cryptic address on a piece of paper and tells a young woman to meet strangers at said location the same evening? I had read enough crime and mystery thrillers to know how this scenario might end.

Nevertheless, I couldn't afford to pass up this opportunity. I was desperate, and this might be my only chance to get any help. So I was going to do my research and be prepared.

I also brought along my pepper spray, just in case.

However, when the shuttle dropped me off at some god-forsaken stop in the middle of nowhere, the alarms in my head went off again. While I had known I'd have to walk, I hadn't expected to travel through such a densely-wooded area. The houses here seemed almost abandoned, for the most part. At least, I thought it would have been a bit more residential.

Still, I stupidly trudged forward, reminding myself about the background checks.

The farther I walked, the fewer homes I saw. The woods thickened. Eventually, the sidewalk ended and street lamps vanished. At this point, I could only see the occasional mailbox at the end of a dirt driveway for homes that were far back off the road.

My map application was telling me that I was in the right place, but could there really be a meeting out here in this remote location? It didn't seem likely.

Unless, Dr. Stephens had faked his background check somehow. It was entirely possible he had lured me out here to murder me.

I was about to turn back when the sound of an approaching motorcycle startled me from my thoughts. Suddenly, it became vital for me to remain unseen. But of course, I wasn't so lucky. My heart raced as the motorcycle pulled to a halt behind me.

"Hey you," a man called. His tone was commanding, though not unkind. But I'd already almost reached my stress limit for the day and the threat of confrontation froze me with terror.

I peeked over my shoulder, unsure of what to do. My already racing heart accelerated as my vision took in the newcomer. The beginning of every horror movie I'd ever watched flashed through my mind.

It was hard not to notice his imposing stature. But as he removed his helmet and shook his head, it was even more impossible to not be entranced by his long, silky locks as they fell gently around his chiseled face.

His movements mesmerized me, and I couldn't seem to pull my gaze away as he used a glove-covered hand to slowly flip his hair back over his shoulder. He was wearing a torn, plaid shirt, extremely faded jeans, and a few days' worth of stubble, and the look worked for him.

I was an idiot, admiring the person who was probably going to kill me. Then again, it was impossible not to watch him. He was so gorgeous that I could almost hear a choir of angels harmonizing in the background. His physique was molded from God himself. His face was perfect seduction. I wanted nothing more than to explore every inch of his smooth, olive skin.

I wasn't stupid. No one that beautiful had good intentions. This was clearly a trap. Much as it normally was in the way of natural selection. This must be how he distracted his victims: dazzling them with his looks. I was certain, because despite all the above, something about this guy screamed *danger*.

There was something off about him. This was as certain as coffee was the greatest beverage known to mankind.

"Do you need any help? This isn't the greatest place for a beautiful young woman like yourself to be wandering around alone." His large green eyes twinkled as he grinned at me, showing off his perfect teeth and adorable dimples. Despite his friendly words, my breath caught. A familiar warning rang in the back of my mind.

Yes, unless I did something drastic, I probably would end up dead. I couldn't let a lumberjack kill me. That would just be ridiculous.

"I'm all right, but thank you," I somehow managed to say. I was barely able to look at him anymore. I'd had just about enough of strangers for the day, and I hadn't even made it to my destination. There was no choice but to move forward; I couldn't turn back, now that he was there.

Maybe if I ignored him, he'd go away.

"Why are you out here?" His deep, melodious voice drifted after me like a caress. I took the risk to glance back again and almost fell to the gravel.

He had gotten off of his bike and was strolling after me as he pushed it beside him.

…Was this for real?

I could probably outrun him, if I had to. I was fast. Despite his attractiveness, he didn't look well off. I doubted that he'd be stupid enough to leave the expensive-looking bike behind just to chase me.

There was also the possibility that I was wrong. Perhaps he was a good Samaritan—albeit a persistent one. If he was going to kidnap me, wouldn't he have done so already?

I slowed down, giving him a wary look. He couldn't be planning on following me the whole way, could he?

He grinned, realizing that he had regained my attention. "I'm just curious. We don't get strangers in this part of town. There's nothing out this way except private residences and trees."

My anxiety rose as I fought to maintain composure. There wasn't a reason for him to *smile* during this discussion. He was totally preying on me. And his words, wasn't that the same as him saying that no one would ever find my mutilated body?

I had to do something. I discreetly searched my purse until I held the tiny can of pepper spray. I was ready. If this guy tried anything—if he even tried to touch me—he would never know what hit him.

"You didn't answer, angel. Where are you headed?" He continued to trail after me, managing to become more persistent with every passing moment. "I can walk you there, just to make sure you're safe."

I stopped walking entirely—I certainly couldn't show up at Damen's with this interloper in tow. "I'm seriously fine." I tried to reassure him in my nicest voice. To show no fear. "You don't need to bother with me. Besides, I don't even know who you are."

"It's not a bother at all." He flashed another blinding smile. "And I guess I should introduce myself. It's a good thing to be wary of strangers. My name is Titus Ducharme. You might have heard of me; I own Jinshu Security."

Never heard of it. I pursed my lips, listening to him continue on. If anything, I was even more suspicious now. I highly doubted that this man was the owner of anything resembling a respectable corporation. He was far too young and too wild.

Titus—if that was his real name—didn't seem to notice. "I'm perfectly legit. You can ask my assistant. But I can't tell you how happy it makes me when I see a young woman asking questions. You have a good head on your shoulders, it would be remiss of me to not see you to your destination."

I raised a brow skeptically, unable to come up with a response. He thought I was smart because I asked a question? It almost sounded as though he was making fun of me.

"Let me take a guess and say that you are headed…" He glanced up and pointed in the direction that I had been walking when he pulled up. "…that way. What a coincidence! I'm going that way as well, so this works perfectly. I'll escort you."

I wasn't sure how to respond. He was being so stubborn. It was time to take some action.

He had at least a foot-and-a-half on me and over a hundred pounds of muscle. I had no chance in hand-to-hand combat. There was only one thing for a woman like me to do in this situation.

Yet, despite my fear, I felt guilty. "Titus—"

He grinned warmly as I said his name, as if he loved hearing the sound. The action made me feel even worse for what I was about to do.

I'd give him one more chance.

"I'm seriously fine." I leveled my most severe glare in his direction, in case he was just a persistent dude with no clue. "You can leave now, please."

He sighed as he rubbed the back of his head, clearly uncomfortable. "I don't think that you understand. These streets…I can't just leave you here alone. I really should—"

Titus didn't see it coming. The second he refused to leave, I pulled out the weapon and aimed the pepper spray right at his eyes.

Once I had downed the attractive stalker, I ignored his screaming and took off like a bat out of hell.

I had only this chance. According to the maps, I was close to my destination. Between my speed and Titus's temporary incapacitation, hopefully he wouldn't catch up to me before I reached safety.

Even if Dr. Stephens sacrificed me in Damen's secret cult-meeting, it was better than a more immediate demise.

The sounds of pained curses grew farther away, but I didn't stop until I had rushed up the winding driveway.

The mysterious address brought me to a massive Victorian home, way past its prime. The lot itself was overrun with foliage. Everything about the place was worn and decrepit, even the wrought iron fence surrounding the visible property and the dirt driveway circling toward the back of the home.

But outside of the ghastly picture, there was something else here too. Something I couldn't see, yet sensed hovering on the edges of my awareness. I couldn't tell what it was, but there was no denying the presence was not of this world.

I never should have come here. But if I left now, I would run into Titus again. And I didn't want that either.

This had to be a mistake. Why would any kind of secret club-like thing meet *here*? Perhaps they were on a job tonight and they were ghost hunting?

That made sense. From the looks of this place, I could see why the owners would call paranormal investigators.

There was only one way to find out if Damen was here, unfortunately. So I forced myself up the cobblestone walkway and across the porch until I stood before a massive door. I felt like an intruder here. But I had been invited…

All I had to do was knock.

I had less choice now than I had in front of Dr. Stephens's office. Before I even had a chance to lower my raised fist, the door swung open. Another man stood there, furiously writing on a clipboard. How he'd known that I was here, I had no idea.

This man, too, was insanely attractive. There must have been something in the water in this part of town. This much handsomeness didn't exist back on campus.

He looked to be a few years older than me. He had a square face and high forehead, and his copper-tinted hair appeared to be sprayed into submission in a tidy wave. Despite the single black hoop hanging from his left earlobe, he seemed professional and stylish. He wore designer jeans and a black dress shirt with sleeves casually rolled up over his massive forearms. And I glimpsed the start of a dark tattoo above his elbow.

I wasn't sure what to make of this—he was almost as large as that Titus guy.

He still hadn't looked up. "You're late again. This is the third time this month. You know that the equipment is still encrypted. I understand your job is important to you, but you can't…"

He glanced up mid-speech, and his voice trailed off. The expression on my face must have been comical, because I hadn't looked away or closed my mouth. Plus, my hand was still posed in the air—having been interrupted pre-knock.

The man's full mouth dipped downward, and he lowered his brown square-framed glasses to study me. "What's this?" He cocked his head to the side as a slow grin appeared on his lips.

I gasped! He had the same exact eyes as Finn. There was no denying their relation. "Damen Abernathy!" I pointed at him triumphantly.

I couldn't believe my excellent turn of luck. After everything that I had gone through to try to find him, I'd finally succeeded.

Now I just needed to figure out everything else.

Damen smirked and all but tossed the clipboard over his shoulder before he leaned against the open door frame. "That would be me." He crossed his arms, biceps bulging against the strain of his shirt. "But I'm not sure I know who you are, or why you are here at my home. However, I am tempted to compromise my morals and find out."

He watched me with an intense look in his eyes, despite his playful words. I had a feeling he was sizing me up. "Very tempted," he repeated. "But as cute as you are, I don't take bribes for grades and—"

"I'm not one of your students," I interrupted him. I didn't need him to get the wrong idea. Plus, really, his *home*? I would have to reserve judgment; maybe it looked nicer inside. I couldn't say anything rude. We were *practically* family, after all. Considering that I one day might be this man's sister-in-law.

"Oh, really?" Damen perked up, and he leaned toward me, closing some of the distance between us. "Then how can I help you, baby girl?" His voice deepened, coming out a seductive purr.

Baby girl? The nickname was terrible, but I still found it hard to breathe under the weight of his attention.

Was it possible that he was flirting with me? I wasn't sure. Something about his presence—his intense demeanor—made it hard to think. Lost in his eyes, my anxiety vanished.

Although I wanted to melt into his smoldering gaze, I held my ground. The semi-prepared speech I had mentally repeated to myself spilled from my lips. "Hello Damen, my name is Bianca Brosnan. I'm Finn's friend. I went to Dr. Stephens's office earlier to look for you because I need your help with…"

"Just a moment." Damen straightened and held up his hand as he stopped me mid-sentence. He was gazing at me with confusion and something else that left me slightly offended.

"What?" I couldn't imagine what could be wrong.

His lips thinned. "Finn has a friend?"

Why were people shocked by this? Finn wasn't all that mean. Everyone had their moments.

I leveled my deadliest glare at him, ready to defend Finn's honor. "Of course Finn has friends! In fact, I'm his *best friend*. I'll have you know that I've been his *best friend* for over ten years."

If anything, my admission seemed to confound Damen even more. But before he had a chance to respond, another man joined us in the doorway.

This new, also unworldly attractive man, was slightly shorter than Damen. However, he was also broader and appeared to be made of pure muscle. I hadn't thought it was possible for any more attractive men to exist in this town. However, that was before this rugged male popped out from behind the previous specimen.

He had an angular face and dark chocolate hair curled away from his eyes. The style accentuated the pure goodness that seemed to pour from his features. His skin was paler than my own light tan, and his expressive brown eyes held an amused but curious glint to them as he looked at me.

"Who's this?" he asked, his slightly-accented voice soothed away the edges of my nerves.

Damen was more subdued than he had been previously as he continued to gaze at me in an unsettling manner. He didn't pause in his inspection as he answered the other man. "This is Bianca. Apparently, she is Finn's best friend."

The other man actually had the nerve to step backward as he put a hand to his heart in shock. "Finn has a friend?"

"I know," Damen replied dryly.

"Stop it!" I frowned at them. If they were going to make fun of Finn, I'd leave. "Don't make fun of him."

No wonder Finn didn't talk to his brother. Haunting or no haunting, I was darn loyal. If the ghost killed me as a result of this, it was a necessary price to pay. Clearly, there would be no help from these two.

The newcomer seemed to know what I was thinking. Before I had a chance to move, he had leapt fully onto the porch and grabbed my hand. "I'm sorry."

I tensed—startled by his unexpected touch. This was almost worse than being stalked on the street by Titus. Than even my fear of the unknown.

"It's not every day Finn…befriends a person," he continued in his deep, rough voice. Despite myself, I felt the tension melt away. "We didn't mean to make fun of him—or you. Please, forgive us."

Damen made a scoff-like sound and raised his eyebrow at me.

"That being established, let's get better acquainted." He smiled slightly, and Damen shot him a curious look. But the new hottie ignored him. "We can pretend that none of this happened. I am Miles Montrone. And you are…" He paused, expecting an answer.

There was something odd about this whole situation. Outside of my initial reaction, something instinctual—almost peaceful—inside of me began to uncurl. Perhaps I could trust this Miles person. He seemed sincere.

"Bianca Brosnan," I responded after a moment. There was no going back, was there?

Miles's smile grew bolder, and I felt as though something significant had just happened. But I had no idea what. "Damen seems to have forgotten his manners. Cultured people shouldn't hold meaningful conversations in doorways. Won't you come in?"

He tugged me gently after him into the house, and I could only silently follow. My stomach clenched—expecting panic at the movement. Normally, I would be fighting the urge to flee if a stranger grabbed my hand. But, surprisingly, nothing happened.

I wasn't sure what was going on, but I was both confused and entranced.

Perhaps it had something to do with the comforting tone of his voice. It was odd I'd feel at ease around these two strangers. But they both seemed normal enough.

And, surely, talking to them would be better than letting the ghost haunt me.

Chapter Three

Impeccable

I wasn't sure how I ended up in this situation, but the entire thing was extremely bizarre.

The house did, indeed, look much nicer on the inside. In fact, I found myself sitting on a plush chaise in the middle of a grand parlor. Damen was alone with me now, as Miles left to get refreshments from the kitchen.

My host had paused his flirting with me since hearing of my friendship with Finn. Instead, he retrieved his clipboard and used his crossed leg as a table while he wrote furiously. Miles had mentioned that there was one other person in the home, but he was busy in the *library*.

Because that was exactly what this place needed.

I wasn't sure what I'd expected Damen Abernathy's private residence to be like, but this was not it. First, there had been the shocking decay of the exterior, but the interior was decked in modern Victorian style. The room was lit by the crystal chandelier and the roaring fire burning in the marble fireplace.

The atmosphere soothed my fear of being chopped into pieces and buried in the woods. Or worse—eaten.

Perhaps Dr. Stephens really was a kindly professor trying to help. All in all, I was beginning to feel more at ease than I had in a long, long time. Well, except for one thing.

Every so often, Damen Abernathy would glance at me in the most peculiar way. It was starting to get on my nerves.

When he did it again—the third time in less than three minutes—I couldn't take it anymore.

"I'm sorry, but have I offended you somehow?" My voice broke through the silence.

Damen almost jumped out of his chair in surprise. It would have been comical if not for the fact that he had somehow managed to make the ungraceful movement look sexy. I was almost jealous—I'd never be able to practically fall on my face in such a manner.

After a moment, he regained his composure. "I beg your pardon?"

So, he was going to pretend that there was nothing wrong? I didn't like that. I couldn't let our relationship start out this way. I had to make an effort. "I said, I'm sorry. I know it was rude of me to just show up, but Dr. Stephens said that…"

"There's nothing wrong with you." Damen waved off my concerns as he removed his glasses and leaned back in the chair. "I'm wondering why *Finn*, of all people, would keep you secret. He's plotting something."

So it wasn't me?

"I'm sorry," I repeated, turning away. Perhaps this was a bad idea. Finn hadn't even told his family about me—there must have been a reason. Maybe he was ashamed? I wasn't exactly the most normal person around.

Even so, it hurt. Besides my parents, Finn had been my whole life. I hadn't realized how little of an impact I'd had in his. He'd gone out of his way to not mention me. Being here was even worse than I'd imagined; he would be beyond furious.

He could never know.

"Finn would never do anything bad," I told Damen, forcing cheerfulness into my voice. "I wouldn't worry."

Finn had told me I was a terrible liar, but I had to try. All I had to do was to control my nerves—once shot, the filter between my mouth and brain tended to fade. "But speaking of that, he doesn't know I'm here. I don't want to bother him. It might make him angry—"

"What do you mean, *angry*?" Damen's gaze narrowed and his voice had turned hard. "Who is *he* to dictate where you can and cannot go? As far as I am aware, Finn doesn't own you or anyone else."

Curse my mouth.

I panicked, waving my hands in front of me in an effort to calm this disaster. "That's not what I meant," I said. The last thing I wanted to do was to cause more conflict between the two of them. "I know that you don't talk. Finn is just protective. I have issues. Finn cares—he looks out for me."

There. Now he'd see what a good guy Finn was.

Damen was silent but didn't appear to be convinced. However, as our eyes met, his cynicism returned to intrigue. I never looked at people this intensely. It seemed invasive. But something about his gaze wouldn't allow me to look away.

I should have been nervous, but it wasn't like that. Instead, a sense of familiarity swelled inside of me—blossoming the longer our gazes locked. My cheeks burned under his scrutiny. There was no way to deny that I was attracted to him.

He stared at me in the same manner. I had no idea what might be going through his mind. Whatever it was, though, seemed to make him frown even more.

I was a crappy future sister-in-law.

The moment between us shattered as Miles popped open the double doors and entered the room, pushing a silver cart. Another man followed him in—probably the person who had been hiding in the library.

The stranger spotted me and his sensual lips quirked up. Something about

33

his expression had me mentally groaning as I realized that I was faced with yet another fantastically attractive man. My heart couldn't take this. My brain couldn't take this. What were the odds of there being so many good-looking men in one place?

Where should I look? When you had your soulmate, you were supposed to forsake all others. To avoid temptation, I might need to gouge out my eyes. Nowhere here was safe.

A moment later—when the new guy spoke—I realized the flaw with my plan. His voice was as beautiful as his face. *Heaven help me.*

"Bianca." He elegantly strode toward me and kissed my knuckles. "It is wonderful to meet someone new. And if Dr. Stephens sent you to us, then you must be quite special. My name is Julian Kohler. I'm sorry that it took so long for me to join you. I hope Damen behaved himself, as he tends to be a flirt."

Damen made a strange noise, and Miles smirked as he set out a fragile-looking tea set. I hardly had the capacity to feel self-conscious at their reactions, because most of my attention was now focused on Julian.

He was taller than Damen, and leaner, with striking blue eyes. His dark complexion was offset by his baby blue polo shirt, and his exposed arms showcased lean muscle. But Julian's most defining characteristic was his long legs—which seemed to go on forever.

He was easily the most beautiful man that I had ever seen in my life. Where the others were rugged or seductive, this man was pure grace.

But he claimed Damen was a flirt? Because I was sure that they all were.

My eyes began to water, and I realized that I had been staring. And I hadn't even responded to his introduction. Not that he had said anything about that, though. Julian just held my hand as if being stared at wordlessly was a normal experience for him.

"I'm sorry," I squeaked out in horror. My cheeks heated at how rude I was being. "It's nice to meet you. And I'm sorry about intruding on your meeting tonight."

"Hush." He pet my hand in a reassuring manner before he sat beside me on the chaise. "It's quite all right. Generally, these meetings are boring, so you are bringing some excitement into an otherwise tedious evening."

I wasn't sure how to respond. But thankfully, he didn't seem to notice. Instead, he made himself comfortable while Miles hovered about, offering me cookies and tea.

Damen, who had regained his composure, rested his chin on his hand and leaned forward. "Dr. Stephens isn't the type to match-make. So, why don't you explain why Dr. Stephens sent you to this meeting, and we'll take it from there?"

Origins

Chapter Four

Evaluation

I should have been able to launch right into my confession—it was what I'd come here to do, after all. But I hadn't planned past getting here. I'd been too worried about being sacrificed.

However, now I was in a pickle. I couldn't tell them *everything*. I had learned that lesson a long time ago. I had to tell them enough so they'd agree there was a problem and they could help me.

Besides, who wanted to admit to cute guys that your ankle had been grabbed while you were bathing the night before? I didn't need anyone to imagine me naked and barf on my account. That would be horrifying.

"It's embarrassing," I stalled, trying to find the words. I had to make this sound as normal as possible—or normal enough for a group of ghost hunters to believe. "And it sounds stupid…"

Julian's mouth dipped at my hesitation, but it was Miles who spoke as he reached across the table and put a warm hand on my knee.

"Sorry to interrupt," he said. "You appear to be a shy person. It probably took a lot of courage for you to come here, seeking help from strangers. It was brave of you to come. Please don't worry. We won't judge you. Just talk to us."

His gaze was too distracting. I folded my shaky hands in my lap and focused on my tea so I could think. "I know it sounds unreal, but hear me out. There's a ghost at the home that I'm watching for my professor.

Strange things have been happening. They started haunting me the first night that I was there, but I can't leave. I told my professor that I'd take care of things."

"Why look for *me*?" Damen asked when I paused. I glanced up to notice he was watching me. As our gazes met, he grinned. "I mean, you are welcome to do so—for any reason, really. I'm not one to argue when a beautiful girl seeks me out. But what made you look for *me* when faced with a paranormal situation?"

Of course he'd ask that. "Finn mentioned that you were interested in paranormal research."

"That's odd." Damen frowned pensively. "You said he'd be angry that you came to see me. Then why—"

"He didn't tell me to come. He mentioned it in passing a while back," I responded. "Finn and I meet every evening. Yesterday, I mentioned asking for your help, and he said it was unnecessary."

"Why would it be unnecessary?" Miles interjected, squeezing my knee as he spoke. The calm his touch instilled surprised me, and I nearly missed what he said next. "Would we be in the way of his work?" he asked. "Was he going to take care of the issue himself?"

What a strange question. Besides, wasn't it obvious? If Finn had been willing to help, then I wouldn't be here. But we were getting off topic.

"Not exactly," I continued. "In any case, I wasn't sure what to do next. So I decided to see you as a last resort. I mean—it's trying to kill me."

Damen started to say something, but Julian held up his hand—cutting him off. Miles ignored both of them and recaptured my attention. "Why do you say that? Why do you think it's a ghost?"

Did this mean they believed me?

That little bit of encouragement was all that I needed. I put my teacup on the table and held my hands together in my lap. Someone was going to listen without judgment. Someone was going to help!

I forced myself to explain before I lost my nerve.

"It's obviously a ghost." I tried to keep my tone even—clinical. "The rooms have cold spots. But there are also noises around the house. Most of the time metallic banging, or sometimes scratching."

My skin broke out in goosebumps as I recalled the next events.

"Sometimes I feel as though I'm being touched," I admitted. "Different places—my legs, arms, and back mostly. But sometimes it's my hair, and…stuff like that." Just the recollection scared me, and I began to pick at the loose threads of my sweater.

Julian noticed and held my hand in a reassuring manner. "There's no reason to be nervous. You're safe here—no ghost to worry about."

I stared at him incredulously—what kind of ghost hunter was he?

"Are you sure about that?" I muttered under my breath, recalling the familiar sensation outside of this structure. It hadn't been evil, but there was no way that this property was haunt-free.

Julian's hand jerked in response. "What do you mean?"

…And again, my mouth.

"Never mind." I shrugged. If they were any good at their jobs as ghost hunters, they would figure it out themselves. If not, then it wasn't my problem.

…But what if *they* needed help? Perhaps I could mail an anonymous letter.

"It does sound like a haunting." Miles glanced at Damen.

Damen nodded, his face solemn. "Is there anything else that has stood out to you?"

They believe me? I hoped that this wasn't a trick, but in case they did…

"Two nights ago," I continued, "I woke out of a sound sleep. I couldn't breathe. And when I tried to get up, I couldn't move either. Also, items have been moved around after I leave a room. For example, the dishes in the kitchen were displaced overnight."

I didn't need to go into details, but I probably should mention the ladder...

With my left hand, I touched my sore jaw, reflexively. "It's been escalating. And it's only been two days."

Julian released my right hand, and I didn't have time to feel the loss before he grasped my left hand instead. I wondered what he was doing. He moved it from my face and touched my chin.

"Is that how you got this bruise?" he asked. His studied my face with a concerned gaze as he nudged me to turn toward him.

My face burned under his scrutiny—I hadn't meant to draw their attention to it. I hadn't even realized my foundation job was so terrible. "I thought that I covered it..."

"That's not what I asked." His deep eyes examined my chin clinically, and his fingers pressed on the area lightly, causing me to flinch. "When did you get this bruise? Did you fall?"

"It's not a big deal. I'll be fine." I tried to pull back, but his steady grip held me in place. After a second, I gave up. "It was an incident with the ghost. I fell off a ladder."

Why were they so concerned? They didn't know me, and I was *trying* to be nonchalant. No one would ever question after the first time, but he hadn't stopped...

Even Finn wouldn't have pressed so much. But granted, he also wasn't the most observant person in the world.

"You fell?" Damen asked, his tone sharp. He sounded angry. "You might as well explain *exactly* what happened. Julian isn't going to let it go. If he sees an injury, he's relentless. It's in his nature—he's in medical school."

I supposed it made sense. "I was working in the conservatory and something pulled the ladder out from under me. I smacked my chin on the table."

Damen glanced at Julian. "Did she break anything?"

Were they serious? It was just a bruise. I was clearly fine, there was no need to fuss. I'd only brought it up so they'd have physical proof of this haunting. The fact that they felt the need to hover around me, concerned about my well-being, left my stomach churning with unease. I wasn't used to this kind of attention.

Julian smiled softly at me before he answered Damen. "It's just a bruise," he echoed my thoughts. "A bad one, but it'll heal. We should ice it though."

"I'll get some," Miles said, jumping to his feet and exiting the room.

Meanwhile, Julian released my face and turned to Damen. "It's already escalating into physical attacks. It might be more than a poltergeist."

Damen was taking notes again and didn't look up as he answered. "True. Generally speaking, a poltergeist doesn't *seek* to harm people directly. Most of their actions are attention-seeking."

"Not necessarily so," a familiar, elderly voice said. I glanced away from Damen, startled to see Dr. Stephens standing at the opened doorway. He nodded at me as he entered the room, closing the door behind him. Claiming a seat of his own, he continued. "Poltergeists *can* hurt people, whether it is intentional or not."

"I am aware of that." Damen didn't seem surprised his mentor had arrived. In fact, he hadn't even looked up. "However, if it's been causing other physical issues—such as the inability to move or breathe—that's an indication something more malevolent might be involved. That's why you sent her here, is it not?"

Dr. Stephens finished making his own cup of tea before answering. "No. The reason I sent Miss Bianca here was that not only is she actively involved in a haunting, she also claimed to have *always* been haunted *by* things. Generally, only one such type a person has a *knack* for attracting spirits. This is a trait that makes them stand apart from the everyday populace."

Panic raced through me—I had completely forgotten what I admitted to

Dr. Stephens during my bout of verbal diarrhea. I was such an idiot.

They would know. They would think that something was wrong with me.

Dr. Stephens hadn't sent me here for help—or rather, not any help of the paranormal kind. Damen was a psychologist, and Julian a doctor-in-training. I didn't know what Miles's involvement was, but Dr. Stephens had totally sent me here for an evaluation.

I was probably their training tool.

No one seemed to notice my horror, and Damen still hadn't paused from his notetaking as he responded. "What's your point? There are many mediums, sensitives, or whatever you want to call them in the world. We already know they tend to become a target more often than not."

"Think, Mr. Damen." Dr. Stephens sounded exasperated. "She's clearly something of the sort, and she just *happens* to be friends with your brother. You're smarter than this."

Damen's pencil froze in midair, and he slowly raised his eyes until they met mine.

My mind was reeling from confusion. Did they believe me, or didn't they? Was this some kind of practical joke?

The tension in the room seemed focused entirely on me, and I wanted to flee. But there was nowhere to run and no way to make an escape. Instead, I concentrated on picking at an imaginary thread on my shirt, trying to keep my hands from shaking.

"What does Finn have to do with anything?" I said. I didn't like this change in topic one bit—what happened to discussing the haunting? This was dangerous territory, and not something I ever wanted to address with others. "Stop joking. The fact that I'm his friend—or that I may or may not see ghosts—has nothing to do with this. Finn doesn't even believe in the paranormal. He says that ghosts don't exist. It's a subject he is extremely passionate about."

The other inhabitants of the room seemed to find my statement to be hilarious.

I couldn't breathe.

They were laughing at me. Laughing at the frustration and self-doubt I faced every day. Laughing about every time my best friend told me I was crazy.

My vision blurred as I got to my feet. I'd had enough of people not taking me seriously.

"It's not funny!" Despite my inner turmoil, my voice was firm. The laughter died as suddenly as it had begun, but it wasn't enough. "You don't know what it's like to live like this my whole life, and to have no one on my side. And now you're all acting as if it's a joke that my best friend says I need to be committed because of the things that I feel. It's *not* funny."

All traces of humor were gone from their faces now.

Before I could say anything else—or leave—Julian grabbed my hand again. "Wait, what did Finn say?"

"It doesn't matter." They didn't need to know. They had already heard more than enough and only seemed to care about Finn now. "If you aren't going to help me, then I'll just leave."

"Bianca." Julian's grip tightened and his eyes earnestly sought out mine, but I turned away. I didn't want to be pulled into the strange hypnotic crap they were able to cast over me.

He sighed. "Bianca, of course we'll help you. But first, please tell us—what did Finn say? We really need to know. What happened?"

No, they really didn't need to know. And there was no way I could open myself up to that kind of humiliation and judgment—not again.

"Never mind." I twisted my arm and Julian let go at once. "I'll just take care of it myself. You can forget I was ever here."

I could feel their gazes on me, following my movements as I gathered up my purse and made for the door. "I'm sorry to have bothered you. Thank you for the tea."

Someone moved behind me, and Damen called my name. But I ignored him. There was nothing else to be said on the matter.

I opened the door, about to step into the hallway, when I came face-to-chest with my giant, lumberjack stalker.

He actually followed me here? How persistent. I didn't need this!

"Titus." Damen was right behind me. "What in the world happened to your face?"

Titus—and apparently that was his real name—looked at me curiously with those striking eyes of his. And even though his face was blotchy, and his eyes watery and swollen, he was still as seductive as before.

How in the world was it even possible?

Despite my admiration of his physical attributes, my heart thundered in my chest in fear. Not only was this man apparently Damen's friend, but I had also *maced* him.

Sure, he had been extremely creepy. But it was different now. No longer was he a random stranger on the street.

I was totally going to get the crap kicked out of me.

"You were coming here?" Titus addressed me, ignoring Damen. "Why didn't you just say so?"

Surely there was a witty response, but I couldn't think of it. My mental limit for the day had been reached, and all I knew was that I was about to receive swift retribution.

"Titus?" Julian approached as well, sounding worried.

This was very bad. Soon they would all know what I had done. And when that happened, they'd think I was even weirder than before. Plus, they would certainly be angry. Of course they would; friends *should* always defend each other.

44

Titus frowned and reached for my shoulder, the very thing I had been terrified of from the first time I saw him. The edges of my vision blacked. So, I did the only thing left for a sensible young woman to do in this kind of situation.

I kicked him in the balls and hightailed it out of there.

Origins

Chapter Five

Stalked

I wasn't sure if the guys—other than Titus—were adept at tracking, so I had no choice but to change my escape route. It was only after I had arrived at the bus stop—covered in burdocks—that I realized it would be obvious I would end up here anyway. So really, my painful trek through the woods had been for nothing.

It was not my brightest moment.

However, by the grace of God, no one had come after me. Not even for revenge for Titus's crushed balls. I only hoped that their lack of response didn't mean they were planning something far more sinister.

I wouldn't have been terribly concerned if it had just been the others— Miles, Julian, Dr. Stephens, or even Damen. The worst they'd probably do would make fun of me, or lock me in an insane asylum. That, I could handle.

No. It was Titus who worried me the most. There was something unsettling about him—and it scared me witless. It also didn't help once I realized that if he hadn't lied about his name, then maybe he was telling the truth about everything else too.

A *security company*, he'd said. I remembered reading things on the internet and in romance novels—stories about corrupt security companies with ties to the Mafia.

He seemed like the type to belong to the underworld. All he needed to do was switch out the plaid with leather.

And his apparent involvement with the group gave me pause. I didn't want to be judgmental, but really—my life on the line. Every survival instinct that I possessed recoiled at his presence.

Besides, the others had laughed at me. I couldn't trust any of them.

But at least it seemed like they were going to let me flee with the remainder of my pride intact.

My relief was short-lived. I wasn't back at my professor's home for even an hour before Miles and Titus arrived.

The fact they knew how to find me so quickly reinforced my theory—Titus was dangerous. Otherwise, how would they know where to find me? Why couldn't they leave me alone?

This was a nightmare. Seeking out Damen had been the worst decision of my life.

As it were, I could only plaster myself behind the security of the front door—terrified for my life. I was caught between being too curious to hide entirely, and too cowardly to make my presence known.

Should I call the police? What would I say? That two paranormal investigators were stalking me outside my front door with a large bouquet of hyacinths to lure me outside so they could kidnap me and sell my organs for profit?

No, they'd never believe me.

However, instead of pounding down the door when it became apparent I wasn't answering, the two of them argued. It was actually an interesting conversation, and I grew brave enough to watch them through the peephole. After all, I had to gather more information on my adversaries.

"You moron. Why are you so stubborn?" Miles said—frustrated, as he tried to convince Titus to return to the car, with no success. "She's going to freak out even more if she sees you!"

"Why would she freak out?" Titus frowned, sounding genuinely confused. "I'm here to apologize." He glanced down at the purple flowers in his hand. "Should I have gotten chocolate, too, do you think?"

Chocolate? I stood on tiptoe, trying to see if he had—actually—gotten a box. But, as he'd said, there was none. Although, as much as I loved chocolate, it probably would have been poisoned anyway. I wasn't that gullible.

Miles scoffed as he pulled out his phone, typing frantically. "First, you stalked the poor girl on the street. Then you overwhelmed her with your scary-ass presence when she was already upset. I'd run away too. If you gave her chocolate, she'd probably think it was poisoned."

"I'm not scary!" Titus argued, placing a hand to his chest. "I'm a friendly guy. Haven't you seen my face?"

"No, you are scary," Miles replied, distracted. "Damen says that there's no record of her cell listed in the school's contact information."

My heart raced. They were looking for my phone number. Not that they'd ever find it—I only had this phone thanks to Finn. Nothing was in my name. But it was the principle—*stalkers.*

Titus still seemed confused, ignoring the fact that his friend tried to pry into the details of my life. "But my secretary says that I'm considered attractive. *Forbes* called the other day, wanting an interview. I don't understand."

So not only was he drop-dead gorgeous, but he was also so modest. Part of me wondered if he was seriously innocent. It might be possible. He did sound harmless—

No, Bianca. I had to trust in my instincts—they were all that I had left. I had to remember that this was a ploy. There was absolutely no way *Forbes* had wanted anything to do with the underworld.

I was no fool.

"You have no idea how women work because you never leave your office. You can't just force yourself into their lives." Miles put his phone away and rang the doorbell again. "Plus, you *can* be both scary and attractive. Just hope she answers the door, or that she's even back here yet. Damen said this was the only professor out on leave. When we see her, we should invite her to dinner. Get her guard down first."

I narrowed my eyes. Only my adrenaline kept me upright. So *that's* how they knew. I should have guessed. Stupid Damen. This was his fault.

Of course I wouldn't answer the door. I was lucky I hadn't turned the lights on before they'd arrived. If I ignored them long enough, they would eventually go away. But I had no intention of going out there.

Get my guard down. They'd have to be insane to believe I would willingly walk to my death.

They bickered for about another hour before it became boring and I snuck away. Despite being criminals that preyed upon young women, they clearly had never mastered the art of breaking and entering.

I lounged around the living room silently for another hour, reading on my phone, before I eventually wandered back toward the front door. They'd apparently given up and left. However, that didn't mean that they weren't hiding somewhere—waiting for me.

About twenty minutes later, my curiosity got the better of me. It had been silent outside for so long there was no way they were still around.

Still, I was wary when I opened the front door.

Nobody jumped out at me, but they hadn't left without making their mark. There—where they had been standing—was the bouquet and a note.

Sorry that Titus is an idiot. Also, I'm sorry that we laughed. We didn't mean to offend you. And we weren't making fun of you—it's complicated. We'll explain later. But we want you to know that you're not alone. We believe you, and we'll help you if you give us a chance. Please think it over and let Damen know.

I frowned in confusion at the weird note. It wasn't fair they'd say it like *that*—dangling acceptance in front of me as bait.

How could they have known I needed acceptance more than flowers or chocolates? It was the only trap I had the possibility of falling into.

Besides all that, what did it even mean to 'let Damen know'? Let him know what—or when? I certainly had no intention of seeing him anytime soon.

Wonderful. Now I had something else to worry about.

It wasn't long before my not-so-friendly ghost-friend decided to come out to play. I had foolishly hoped it had given up because the entire time Miles and Titus were outside, it remained hidden. But it was too good to be true, and I sensed its presence again. Where it was at the exact moment, I couldn't pinpoint.

So now, along with being on edge from feeling of being watched by the house-ghost, I spent the rest of the evening reflecting on the events of the day. Conclusion? I might have overreacted a tiny bit. Probably.

But it didn't matter if I had overreacted. While the guys—sans Titus— might have had good intentions, it would simply be too embarrassing to work with them now. Besides, they obviously had a serious issue with my relationship with Finn—and their attitude really offended me.

I had no other choice. I had to end this haunting without their help. So the day hadn't been a total waste of time, after all.

A *sensitive*, Damen called me. Of course, I tried to look into my abilities in the past, but nothing came up. How had Damen known? Did he know *everything?* Perhaps he was super smart, like Finn. I had to dig into this again. Hopefully, my trip to the library would provide some answers.

With my planned research topic in mind, I finally went to bed.

Something brushed across my awareness—like the sensation of falling in a dream—and I jerked awake, disoriented. I wasn't sure what time it was or how long I had been asleep, but it was still night and the house was quiet.

Everything seemed normal, so why was—

Tap. Tap.

The noise echoed throughout the otherwise silent room. A slight tapping. The sound a knife would make when tapped against a glass. While it wasn't the most frightening thing the residential ghost had subjected me to, there was most certainly an unsettling atmosphere in the room.

Something was different this time.

The small bedroom contained a twin-sized bed. The head of said bed was under the solitary window, which was currently filled with the soft moonlight streaming through the glass. Some feet away from the foot of the bed stood an old vanity. It was low to the floor, and the most distinguishable characteristic was the large, oval mirror affixed to it.

Professor Hamway was a collector of antiques—including small knickknacks. For display on the vanity, she had chosen tiny glass perfume bottles. She was also meticulously tidy, and the various sized bottles were organized on the top of two glass trays.

Other than these items, a houseplant, and a small bedside table, the room held nothing else. Nowhere for anything to hide. And—thanks to the moonlight—I could clearly see I was alone.

Yet, something wasn't right.

I had just pressed my back against the headboard, when the temperature in the room decreased. Again, the tapping echoed throughout the area. It was soft, but close. The sound definitely originated from this room.

My breathing caught, and my fear escalated with every passing second. At the same time, I felt stupid for being afraid—I had decided earlier that I could handle this on my own. I wouldn't be able to do anything acting like this. But I couldn't stop from curling into a ball and pulling the sheet more tightly around myself.

Tap.

This time, I was watching, so I didn't miss the slight movement on the top of the vanity.

One of the bottles had been lifted into the air before being placed into its previous position just as slowly. This time, without pause, another bottle lifted. Another tap.

I had no idea what to do. I wanted to run away, but at the same time, this was the first time I didn't feel hostility. The lack didn't make the situation any less creepy, but it was only that which made me pause.

The scene repeated itself again—a larger bottle this time—when something else caught my attention. A shape, resembling the beginnings of a shadowed figure, began to appear in the reflection of the mirror.

It was barely there—a dark cloud at the bottommost corner of the mirror. In fact, it could have been a trick of the light. But somehow, I knew better.

The bottles weren't touched again. But as seconds passed, the shadowy figure began to grow in size and visibility. It continued to grow until, at one point, it almost passed as the blurred reflection of a child-like figure.

Nope. It was past the time to leave! I moved up in the bed slowly, trying to not draw attention to myself as I uncurled and touched my toes to the wood floor. My slippers were there at the bedside, so I pushed my feet into them and—just as silently—began to inch myself out of the bed.

Sleeping outside seemed like an excellent plan! I just needed to get there without being noticed.

Unfortunately, I only made it to the foot of the bed before a floorboard creaked beneath me, the sound echoing loudly throughout the room. The figure, which had been swaying slightly in front of the mirror, froze.

I couldn't breathe from fear.

A long moment passed, and another. The air became tangible as the atmosphere shifted. While I hadn't been the focus of the ghost's attention before, I certainly was now.

Everything inside of me screamed to run—to hide. Ignoring problems and pretending that nothing was wrong, for me, usually resulted in those issues going away. Following that instinct was how I had survived so far.

But...hadn't I decided earlier I had to figure this out on my own? Nothing was going to change. I'd never learn anything if I kept going on with the status quo.

I had done many things outside of my comfort zone the last couple of days. Why not this? I could muster up the courage to confront this ghost-child directly!

Keeping that in mind, I forced my pounding heart to calm as I took a deep breath. My nerves steadied after a tense moment, and I straightened up from my hunched position.

"Hello." I held out my hand in front of me in a placating manner as I faced the mirror. Trepidation and curiosity thickened the air, but I still wasn't feeling anything hostile from the spirit.

"Are you lost?" I asked.

The room grew impossibly colder, and I shuddered as my breath became visible. Yet the shape didn't move. So I didn't either. I had never had this happen before, so I had no idea what to expect.

A tense moment passed, and I remained still outside of my shallow breaths and shivering. Then, suddenly, a translucent outline formed in the space near the vanity. Still, whatever it was couldn't be powerful, because I was still unable to make out more than the fact that the shape was female.

And she was looking right back at me, just as scared as I was.

Then, the fear retreated as sorrow and grief touched my senses—a mixture of us both. After all, one of the symptoms of my *sensitivity* seemed to be the ability to feel the emotions of the spirits around me.

"It's all right," I told her. I had made the right decision to stay. This spirit, at least, didn't mean me any harm. "Why are you here?"

Even through her indistinguishable features, I knew she was watching me—curious. However, she still made no move to respond.

I frowned, unsure of what to do next. What if she didn't know how to communicate? That would make things more difficult.

She continued to study me for a time before a spike of fear shot through the room. Then she was gone. There was nothing left in her place.

No shadow. No shape.

Nothing.

Just me, watching my own frazzled reflection in the mirror.

Origins

Chapter Six

Research

It was way too early for any sane person to be awake, but I found myself in such a state. It was only through the power of overpriced coffee, and the ghost-child's antics, I remained out of bed.

Instead, I found myself waiting at the coffee shop—counting down the moments before the library opened and I could begin my research.

So someone—a little girl—haunted my professor's home.

Now, more than ever, I was determined to find answers. A child had no business spending their afterlife as a ghost.

The problem was, I really had no idea how to help. Maybe if she reached closure she would move on. My best bet would be to figure out her name. If I could find out if a little girl had died in the house, then everything else might fall into place.

This could be a difficult task; the house was fairly old and had a long history of owners. Its most recent renovation had apparently been the talk of the town, considering the home had been uninhabited before Professor Hamway's husband—an architect and city official—acquired the place.

The fact that Black Hollows was a small town might make my search go more quickly. And also, this home was of particular historic import. If something tragic had happened there, then there must be a record of the event.

To find that information, I would probably have to access the periodical archives—and I had no idea where to begin with that. However, I was willing to bet that Ms. McKinnen—the head librarian—would be able to assist. And that was only if she didn't already know the information off the top of her head.

Ms. McKinnen was a notorious gossip and heavily involved with the local historical society. I would only need to *casually* mention that I was housesitting for Professor Hamway, and Ms. McKinnen would gleefully tell me every horror story that she might know regarding the property. I would be able to cut most of my legwork by just talking to her.

Then there was my second reason for being at the library today. If I truly wanted to help this ghost-girl, then I needed to learn more about my sensitivity and any abilities that gave me—and people like me.

I frowned down at the top of my white coffee cup. Remembering this topic made me recall the events of the night before—

"Bianca?" Finn's shocked voice broke through my thoughts. My eyes shot up. The blond-haired man was pushing past students in line at the coffee shop in order to reach my small, round table. "What are…"

"Hello, Finn." I smiled at him, hoping the guilt from my lies didn't show on my face. "How are you? What are you doing here so early in the morning?"

Finn's mouth dipped, and he didn't respond at first. Instead, he set his leather backpack on the floor and sat down in the seat across from me. "It's not early. And I come here every day—to study. But"—he leveled a suspicious look at me, his gray eyes calculating—"you don't."

I raised an eyebrow in response, but he continued, "I got your message last night. Why did you cancel our meeting? What's going on? I was worried."

Sure. I could tell how worried he was when he didn't even care if the ghost killed me.

I picked up my cup and blew on the rising steam before I answered, trying to sound nonchalant. "I *do* have homework too. Plus, I like reading. It's not unheard of for me to come to the library, you know."

"All right," he conceded as he continued to study me. "But you only come late at night, when most people are partying. In fact, how can you even stand to be awake before ten in the morning?"

Darn him, he was right.

"The magic of caffeine." I sipped on my coffee again, as if to prove my point. "Lots and lots of caffeine."

His lips thinned, but he nodded. From the wary look in his eyes, he knew I was hiding something. But he seemed inclined to let it drop.

Instead, he pulled out his laptop and opened it—ready to do his technology thing.

That was kind of nonsensical. "Finn, why are you setting up? The library opens in less than ten minutes. Won't you just move again?"

"Yes." Finn began typing. "But that's ten minutes worth of work that I've gotten done. I am busy right now, and I'm behind…" His voice trailed off as he frowned at the computer.

He was weird.

"I thought you finished your work for the semester already."

Finn distractively waved his hand. "It's not that. Don't worry, it's nothing that concerns you. I'm working on family stuff. My mother needed me to check into something. Where did you go last night?"

I ignored his question. "Your mom has you doing corporate work?"

"Something like that." He looked up finally, his gaze meeting mine. My heart suddenly jerked—he was displeased. But about what?

After a silent moment, the look passed and he grinned warmly at me. "I'm glad you are here with me," he said. And in an unexpected move, he shut his laptop and pulled one of my hands into his own. "I work better with you around. You inspire me. I don't know what I'd do without you, Bianca."

I almost choked, and my face exploded in heat. This was the side of Finn that always managed to catch me off guard—the one that made me think I meant as much to him as he did to me.

And every time, I acted like an idiot. "I do? I—I'm glad I could help."

"You do." He traced his thumb over my knuckles. My face grew warmer at the action and his grin grew. "We should work together today. Are you going to be in the library all day? Sit with me."

My warm feelings vanished.

I averted my eyes, unable to stand his intensity. He couldn't know what I was researching. "Maybe..."

"*Maybe?*" Finn sounded surprised, and when I looked up, he was watching me with raised eyebrows. After our gazes met, he let go of my hand. "You don't want to sit with me?" He paused, and an expression that I had never witnessed from him before shone in his serious eyes. "Bianca, are you meeting someone else? Have I done something?"

"No!" I vehemently denied, somewhat frightened at the intensity of his reaction. He was being terribly possessive. Especially for someone who had never even asked me on a date. I would have remembered if he had done so, because it was, after all, an event I had been dreaming about for years.

Or, was he only upset because he was afraid I had replaced him as a friend?

I was so confused.

I fidgeted as I tried to think of a way to redirect his attention. "I have research to do today. In fact, I might not even be here all day. I planned on going back and forth between the library and greenhouses."

He rested his chin on his fist as he watched me. "You're a terrible liar. The greenhouses are on the other side of campus, and you're wearing a skirt."

I froze, the fabric he mentioned clenched in my fist. Finn was right, of course. I never wore skirts when working in the conservatory. "Um..."

"What have you been up to—today and last night?" Finn studied me, his eyes demanding answers. "Are you lying to me about something?"

I grew more flustered as the seconds passed. I had to think of something!

He had made his point clear two days ago, and I couldn't bring up *that* topic again. Even outside of meeting Damen, he'd never believe what Damen had said about me being a sensitive. Plus, if he knew I was involved in anything paranormal—especially *trying* to talk to a ghost—not only would he get involved, but so would my parents.

I couldn't go through that confrontation with him again. Even if he—and everyone else—thought it was for my own good. It would break me this time.

So I had to think of something that would guarantee Finn would have zero interest in being anywhere near me today. A topic that would make a male flee in terror. Something awful.

"I—" My mental resources screamed out ideas, but nothing brilliant came to me. Lacking anything else, I blurted out the first thing that came to mind. "I'm doing a research paper on how human placenta usage in gardening may or may not be nourishing to the soil."

Finn's mouth was opened in shock, and my face burned. But I couldn't stop now. "I have a theory that if you grind up the pla—"

"Stop!" Finn's complexion was slightly green as he watched me in horror. "That's great for you, but I really don't need to know anymore. Please."

Crude, but effective. It had worked.

I tried to smile at him as I drove the rest of my point home. "I could still sit with you, if you want. I just think you'd find it gross. I might have to interview the librarian, since they know a lot. I was also going to touch on the topic of using a women's menstra—"

"Just, *please*, stop talking about this. This whole thing. Stop." Finn had buried his head under his arms now. "It's all right. I don't care what Bryce has got you working on, but do your research far, far away from me."

"Oh." I pretended to look sad even though the mention of Professor

Hamway's assistant professor, Bryce Dubois, caused my ire to rise. How would he act when we were married and he had to deal with this fact of life? "If you insist."

"I insist." Finn stood up and gathered his laptop. "The library's open, by the way. Are we still on for tonight?" He grinned at me again. "It's not the same without you."

Tonight? Well, I did have a ghost to bond with. But I could spare an hour or two. "Sure."

Ms. McKinnen had the weekend off, so the bulk of my research would have to wait. I had awkwardly asked the volunteer at the desk, but she had been no help. Besides, I didn't want to make too big of a deal out my search. I didn't want Professor Hamway to hear of any weird tales about me when she returned.

So research on sensitives, mediums and the like had become my agenda for the day.

I moseyed around the library before I found a private cubicle near the cultural reference section and set up base there. Thanks to the prestige of our anthropology and psychology departments, we had an impressive collection of paranormal reading material available.

Unfortunately, hours flew by and the only thing I had gained from my time was a cold mocha latte and even more confusion about the subject matter than when I had begun.

The texts were all theoretical, and information varied based on culture and topic. So, in the end, none of the research had been helpful in gaining an understanding of myself.

Damen probably knew the answers to my questions. However, I had dramatically burned that bridge the day before. But not knowing—and knowing that they *did* know—was making it hard to resist the urge to approach them again. Even if Titus was a lumberjack mafia member, would Damen really let him kill me?

I doodled on the edge of my paper, sighing. I wasn't ready to be brave yet. I'd exhaust all other avenues of information first. Because the fear for my life had lessened, knowing I was dealing with a child, but the embarrassment of seeing them again had not.

But in the end, was my pride worth more than answers?

First, I should check the library in town, and then evaluate my remaining options.

"Are you Miss Brosnan?"

I jumped, almost snapping my pencil in two as I spun in my seat to see who had called me.

I saw an elderly woman a few feet away, wringing her hands. She wore a floral print dress, complete with an old-lady sweater and dark tights. Her white hair was pinned back into a grandmotherly bun, but the style did nothing to tame the flyaways that surrounded her face. She was taller than me, but thin and frail. However, her eyes were sharp beneath her gold-rimmed glasses.

She was probably here to chastise me for sneaking in a beverage, which was technically not allowed.

"I'm so sorry!" I apologized, grabbing my cup as I shot to my feet. "I'll get rid of it right now."

"What?" She seemed confused before she spotted the white container in my hand. "Oh, no dear. I don't care about that."

Now *I* was confused. Why would someone be looking for me in the library? Who was she?

"I heard that you were searching for information on Professor Hamway's

63

home," she said, surprising me. "I grew up in this town. So I know a lot of the city gossip."

"Oh." I stood there for a moment, unsure of what to say. I hadn't been expecting to talk here. Plus, she was old and frail-looking. I should offer her a seat, but these weren't the best chairs. "Um…"

She chuckled before tilting her head. "Come along, dear." She turned and began to slowly hobble away, leaning heavily on her cane.

Now I felt even worse. She had searched the library for me?

She waved her free hand in the air, noticing that I wasn't following her. "We'll have a little chat in my office—just the two of us."

She had an office? I still didn't even know who she was.

"Wait," I called out, rushing to gather my books and papers. Why was I so messy?

As I was shoving everything in my bag, she glanced back at me and her voice changed slightly. "Hurry now."

Oh no, she was getting angry. "Okay, let me just—"

"Ms. Protean, fancy seeing you here." Damen Abernathy's decadent tones reached my ears, causing me to freeze in shock. A silent curse shot through my mind. Somehow, I hadn't been able to avoid his velvety smooth voice and entrancing looks for as long as I had hoped.

I heard something resembling a growl, and I peeked around the cubicle. Damen stood nearby, but I didn't think I was within his line of sight. He was smiling at the elderly woman. She had turned to face him as well, and I noticed her features no longer held grandmotherly softness.

She was glaring at him, but that didn't seem to bother Damen at all as he continued. "It's *so* rare to see you outside of your classroom and office. What brings you here today?"

I wasn't ready for this. I had kicked Titus in the balls. I had also maced him. I needed more time.

Perhaps Damen being here was a coincidence. He might not even be aware that I was here at all. I was still hidden behind a cubicle.

"I'm sorry to interrupt, but I need to borrow Miss Brosnan for a while."

Darn it.

"Why?" Her voice was unexpectedly harsh. "I need her at the moment. We were about to have a discussion."

"That's not such a good idea." Damen's face was still the picture of politeness. "I was looking for you as well, to be honest. Cécile has escaped from your office and is causing havoc in the lunchroom. Brandon attempted to capture her, but he is now being treated in urgent care. As for Cécile, the last I saw, she was perched on the refrigerator and was clawing at the heads of any faculty member leaving or entering the room."

Ms. Protean frowned. "Don't lie. My Cécile is an angel. You must have mistaken her for someone else's vile beast."

"I doubt it," Damen replied, his tone slightly icier. "I believe you are the only faculty member who owns a Persian with a bejeweled collar and pink claws."

"My poor Cécile!" Ms. Protean covered her mouth in horror. "She must be so frightened." She turned to me, apologetically. "I'm so sorry, dearest, but we need to reschedule. I must go before those brutes terrorize my innocent animal again."

Damen raised an eyebrow, looking at her sardonically. She didn't seem to notice. She was already off in a rush—more quickly than I thought possible, based on her appearance.

Damen focused on her retreat—he totally wasn't paying attention to me. This could be my only opportunity for escape. I just needed space to compose myself before the inevitable confrontation.

I grabbed my packed bag and slipped into one of the aisles of bookcases. I had to be quick.

I hadn't even made it ten feet down the narrow aisle before I was pulled to a halt. Damen gazed at me, amused, as he held firmly on to my backpack. "Where do you think you are going, baby girl?"

Chapter Seven

Kidnapped

Even though I struggled, Damen had a firm grip on my backpack and wasn't letting go. I was trying to ignore him, but I'd lost momentum and I slipped backward on the laminate floor. He continued to pull me toward him until my back rested against the hardness of his chest.

I could no longer ignore my predicament. "Damen, *what* are you doing? Let me go!"

Perhaps he was more like Titus than I'd thought, and he needed a dosage of the same deterrent.

He chuckled. "I'm holding you this way so you can't escape. And, also, so you can't attempt any underhanded tricks."

"If you mean what I did to Titus, there was nothing underhanded about that," I retorted. "It was self-defense."

This was the worst. He knew—Titus had tattled on me. And he was angry.

"It was hilarious," Damen said. His voice was a purr next to my ear— making it hard for me to focus. "And well deserved, I will admit. Titus can be overbearing. However, with you, I'd rather play it safe."

Who was overbearing *now*?

"But there's something else to discuss first." His breath was warm against my ear.

I tried to ignore the shivers that shot down my spine as I focused on his words. "What?"

"How do you know Ms. Protean?" he asked. "Why would she need to talk to you?"

His questions caught me off guard, and I turned back to him in confusion. His face was both intense and worried.

"What does that have to do with anything?" I asked.

Damen sighed, releasing my backpack before turning me to face him. I hadn't realized before now I had backed up to the end of the narrow aisle and was trapped between the edge of the bookshelf and his larger frame.

It should have been intimidating. Instead of being scared, I was only flustered. I couldn't imagine why, because the only other person whoever made me feel this way was Finn…

Damen didn't seem to notice my discomfort. "Ms. Protean," he repeated. "What does she want with you?"

What was it to him, anyway? Did he loathe grandmotherly figures or something? But he seemed so concerned that I couldn't get offended at the question. "She said she was going to help me. I was looking for some information."

Damen gave me an appraising look. "Without me?"

Why did he have to seem so smug about this? It was as if he knew the effect he had on me. I opened my mouth to respond with something witty—which would probably have been embarrassing anyway—when the sounds of laughter drifted over from the next row.

The noise shattered the enchantment that had been cast over us, and my face burst with heat. There was no question as to how ridiculous we'd look to any passerby. The library was no place for games!

Damen's gray eyes glinted mischievously—he must have had the same realization.

"Damen, let me go," I hissed at him. But this only encouraged him, and he smiled, causing my heart to beat faster. "Someone is going to come down here and see us!"

"Really?" His grin grew wider. "So it's all right if we don't get caught, baby girl? Consider it noted."

"No!" My mind screamed even though my words were a hiss. "You can't play games with students. This is inappropriate. You are basically a professor."

"Ah." He ran his finger down my cheek. "But you aren't my student." His mouth dipped slightly. He tilted his head as his gaze continued to hold mine. "There's just something about you."

"Why are you so annoying?" I gritted out, trying to save face. Plus, was he kidding me with this? That sounded like a line from a cheesy romance novel. How many times had that worked for him in the past?

Finn's stupid, horny brother. He could go flirt with someone else. No matter how much I wanted to lean into his touch, or melt under his scorching gaze—I wanted to poke him in the eyes that much more. What a quandary.

The sound of my name being called by a familiar voice saved Damen from getting hit where it hurt.

I tore my attention from Damen as I glanced in panic at the end of the aisle. This was the worst possible thing to happen. Finn could *not* know I was talking to his brother.

Finn called my name again, closer now. He was going to find us…

Damen, in the meantime, glanced over his shoulder—toward the direction of Finn's voice. He frowned, muttering, "God, he still sounds like a douchebag. And not an ounce of courtesy, like he owns the place." He didn't seem all that concerned.

"Will you stop saying mean things?" I couldn't stop the hysteria. "This is a disaster. Finn can't find out I *know* you!"

Origins

"Why?" Damen's eyes returned to me, flashing with something new. "Because you think he'd get angry?"

I didn't think—I *knew*. And my heart raced at the thought.

There was a note of challenge in Damen's voice, but there was something else too. It was almost as if he was hurt. It made me feel guilty on top of my fear. I had never wanted to hurt his feelings.

What was wrong with me?

I was just about to apologize, when he continued speaking—studying my face. "I'll have you know my *little brother* doesn't scare me."

What did this mean? I was still trapped at the end of the aisle between him and the bookshelves. Finn could find us there at any second, and Damen didn't seem to care. When that happened, Finn would not only know I had disregarded his wishes, but that I hadn't listened to him about the *other topic* as well.

Every worst-case scenario flashed through my mind, and my breathing sped up.

"But he does scare you," Damen said suddenly.

I blinked, his words crashing through my agonized thoughts. I was so fixated on Finn I had completely forgotten Damen was even there. Watching me.

He didn't look very happy either—his face a mask of concern and fury. "Something stupid like this, and you're afraid that you might anger him. What did he do to you?"

Oh no. No, no, no.

My eyes widened as I looked up at him. "I'm not scared," I explained. "I'm just trying to prevent a confrontation. Can we leave, *please*? Before he finds us?"

Finn called out to me again. He had to be only seconds away from finding us.

I flinched. We had to move *now*.

"Liar." Damen tore his gaze from mine and grabbed my hand. He seemed to have made up his mind. Stunned at his sudden action, I ended up just following along.

He pulled me after him, quickly approaching an opening between the bookcases to an adjacent doorway reserved for the library staff.

"I'll help you," he said, pulling me behind him. "But rest assured, we will be discussing this later. You deserve better than this."

How…caring?

There wasn't anything to do at this point but allow him to lead me through various hallways and down staircases until we exited the building. Damen pulled me after him into the faculty parking lot.

We were safe. But *now* where was Damen leading me?

"Wait." I tugged my arm, but Damen's grip was solid. He did, however, stop walking.

"Where are we going?"

He shot me an incredulous look. "Unless I'm mistaken, you said you didn't want Finn to know you were with me. Am I right?"

"Yes, but I'm still with you," I pointed out. "So, you are now kidnapping a university student. That won't look good on your resume."

One of his eyebrows shot up, and I mentally chastised myself for finding the action attractive. "Kidnapping?" he asked, amused.

"Yes." I pointed at him with my free hand. "Don't think I don't know what you are up to. You still have revenge on your mind. Titus had it coming. What else was I supposed to do?"

Damen's mouth twisted into a grin before he dropped my arm, turning to face me fully. "I know he had it coming, and I'm glad."

I continued, arguing my point. I'd never admit I was wrong about what I'd done to Titus! He was harassing me! "I don't regret it—" Then his words penetrated through my thoughts. "What?"

"A woman walking through an unknown neighborhood alone. If someone like Titus wouldn't back off, then I'd have maced him too." Damen was still grinning.

I frowned, recalling the secondary wrong I performed toward the aforementioned man. "But… I kicked him in the…male parts too," I whispered.

Damen seemed as if he was about to burst out laughing. "Yes, but you were already uncomfortable. Plus"—he leaned in toward me and touched my nose with his finger—"it *was* funny. Actually, you fit in our group quite well. It'll be helpful when we work together."

I jerked back, covering my face with my hands. I couldn't handle this much…flirting. That was what it was, right? I didn't even know.

So this meant I wasn't going to die? The mafia wouldn't torture me for my wrongs? Still, Titus had to hate me. That hadn't been a nice thing for me to do to him.

"How are…," I trailed off, unsure of what to say. 'Titus's balls' would have been crude, so I went with the next best phrasing. "How is Titus doing?"

Damen flung an arm over my shoulders as he led me through the parking lot. Now that I knew he wasn't angry with me, I didn't protest. For some reason, he seemed to want to hang out with me.

But since my panic abated, all I could focus on was him. The warm feeling of his arm over my shoulders. The way he towered over me, making me feel so small. And he radiated a comforting, musky scent that seemed to surround me.

He was nicely dressed too. He was scholarly, with his glasses and oxfords. His tweed jacket was tailored to his powerful form. Everything about his appearance seemed expensive.

I wondered how much money forensic psychology student-teachers made.

I probably looked out of place next to him, even though I wore one of my nicer pleated skirts and sweaters. Somehow, I had a feeling that all of these guys had a different budget than that of a regular student/post-graduate.

This disparity could be a problem if I was going to be around them for any length of time. I would need to improvise.

The train of thoughts screeched to a halt as I came to my senses. I wasn't *going* to be hanging around them, even if they weren't going to try to kill me after all. This entire situation was way too awkward. And I hadn't even accepted their help.

Yet.

Although, it was tempting.

But there was one more matter—besides Finn—that had been picking away at my subconscious. "Wait."

Damen paused, glancing down at me.

It was difficult to not be lost in his eyes, but I persevered. "I forgot. You laughed at me. I'm not your science experiment, you know."

His brows furrowed. "What are you talking about?"

Darn him for looking so befuddled. It was too adorable. "I know all about you being a psychologist," I said. "I won't be your new lab rat."

Damen's mouth twisted. "Do you always jump to wild conclusions?"

I gasped, offended. "Of course not! Life has proven that my conclusions are very logical."

"Really?" He frowned—my response seemed to have displeased him even more. "First of all, I'm a *forensic psychologist*. I work with the police on a specialized task force. I'm not involved in clinical psychology or counseling."

His gaze was still serious as he studied me, as if he wanted me to truly understand his words. "And secondly," he continued, "despite what you have been led to believe, you aren't crazy. We weren't laughing at *you* at all. We were laughing at Finn because he's an idiot. Maybe one day you'll learn how much of an idiot he is. But rest assured that there is *nothing* wrong with *you*."

But no one has ever believed me…

"You aren't the only *special* one out there, baby girl." Damen grabbed my hand, and I followed along passively as he continued. "Not by a long shot."

I found myself back at Damen's house again under much different circumstances than the day before. I wasn't a stranger showing up on his front porch this time, but had been invited over instead. Sorta. In either case, today it was easier for me to feel relaxed. And his house was warm, cozy today. As soon as we'd arrived, he lit a fire, grumbling about the cooling weather and lengthening days.

There were a myriad of questions ready to spill from me. Questions such as: 'Why had Damen meticulously restored the interior of his home, but left the outside of the property and grounds unattended?' Or: 'Why was he living in the middle of a creepy forest?' It would be rude to ask.

Despite proprieties, I *needed* to know—otherwise, I would start drawing my own conclusions. And that, sometimes, wasn't the best.

"Damen?" I studied the room, wondering how to word this in a kind way. "Why does your home have a Transylvanian vibe to it?"

He was sipping tea in a seat across from me and paused as he shot me a perplexed look. "What in the world do you mean by that?"

Okay, so maybe this atmosphere wasn't weird for him. Perhaps this was his normal.

After all, Damen had been the one who told me that I *wasn't alone*. Perhaps he was paranormal and this was how he was accustomed to living. An elegant being, hidden away in grandiose finery amongst crumbling ruins.

I contemplated for a moment. It was still daylight. Was it possible that he was a vampire?

"Stop that right now," he interrupted my train of thought with a keenly perceptive look. "I'm a regular person—just as much as you are."

I stared at him in shock. How had he known what I was thinking?

"Your every thought shows on your face." Damen put his teacup on the table and leaned in toward me. "Plus, you basically brought up vampires. It wasn't a leap for me to figure out what you were thinking. I'm already pretty sure I know the kind of person *you* are."

"You said that you weren't going to analyze me!" I said, indigent.

"I'm not analyzing you," he responded with a smug look. "I'm stating a fact. You appear to be passive and quiet, yet come up with such eccentric conclusions. It's easy to see you have a vivid imagination."

He tilted his head as I pouted, and the light from the fireplace reflected back from his intense gaze. "You don't need to explain, but I can't figure out how *you* are friends with Finn."

I pursed my lips—this was not a good topic.

After a moment of silence, he seemed to have gotten the message because he just sighed. "Even so. I'd like the chance to be your friend too. You seem to trust Finn, so do you think you could trust me?"

My breath caught. He knew some of my weirdness, and he still offered. In fact, he knew more about me than I did at this point. And after everything that happened yesterday, he didn't judge me. Instead, he wanted to be my *friend*.

Why would he want to be my friend?

I didn't understand the offer, even though I wanted it so much. I wasn't sure how I'd keep this friendship from Finn, but I desperately needed it.

I should decline. There was no way this would end well, not with my history. However, when I opened my mouth to speak, I heard myself saying, "That would be wonderful," instead.

Chapter Eight

Sound

"Excellent. Then it's done," Damen smiled. He sat back in his seat, a confident air about him. "That being the case, we'll get started right away. Is tonight good? Yes. We'll all come over to Professor Hamway's house with you. I'll even have Julian pick up some Chinese food."

I wasn't sure what to say.

He raised an eyebrow. "You don't like Chinese? That's a shame. I was excited for moo goo gai pan. Well, pizza is fine too, I suppose."

What in the world was he talking about? I blinked at him, stunned. "But—"

"We're friends now. You don't want to be?" He seemed genuinely worried that I'd change my mind.

No, I *did* want to be friends, but…I nodded numbly in response.

He flashed me a triumphant grin. "Well, friends don't let friends get haunted by vengeful spirits. We have a ghost to hunt."

My finger was in the air in protest, even though I had no idea why. I didn't even know what I could say. I had wanted help and planned on asking…again. One day. But this—it almost felt as though I had been outmaneuvered in some way.

"So, baby girl—" Damen sounded smug, all of his attention focused on me.

I squirmed under the attention. What did he want? Plus, he was still using that nickname. If I was going to be his friend, I didn't think it was appropriate for him to be calling me 'baby girl'.

"What kind of sensitive *are* you?" he asked. His tone was flirty, but his gray eyes had turned serious.

Again, his bluntness stumped me. He was just moving right along, wasn't he?

I wasn't sure how to answer, because I really didn't know much of anything about my sensitive nature…

"I don't know," I admitted. "I didn't even know there was a term for it before. I thought that I was just cursed…"

I was so embarrassed. How pathetic was it that this was something I'd always had but knew next to nothing about?

"Well, you aren't cursed." Damen seemed to be thinking. "There's nothing wrong with not knowing, either. There's a lot of misinformation out there. And even if you did know, it's easy to become confused. Tell me about your experiences, and we'll see what we can figure out."

I wasn't sure how this was relevant to the haunting, but whatever. He seemed to know what he was doing.

"I mostly get a feeling…" I paused, trying to decide how to describe this in a relatable way. "As if you are in a pool of murky water, and something brushes up close to you. It's that feeling you get when you know you're not alone."

Damen hummed, writing in his notepad, and glanced up. "That's a good analogy, actually. Most sensitives can only say that they just *know*. Can you see the spirits? If so, do you have to do anything in order to communicate with them?"

"Not all the time." I pulled at my hem as I recalled past instances. "Not like I used to…"

My words trailed off, and he inclined his head—encouraging.

I sighed, not wanting to get into this. It wasn't like I thought he wouldn't believe me. It was the topic itself that made me uncomfortable.

And was it really necessary for me to have to go into this much detail and reveal my deeply seated quirkiness with a man I barely knew? After all, he had enough problems just dealing with Finn…

"I don't do anything to cause it to happen," I said. "But I had always been able to see shapes, figures, shadows…In most instances, they appeared like people. I could talk to them if I wanted. But I tried not to. Then some stuff happened—and it wasn't the same after that. The hauntings only recently started up again when I took on this house-sitting job at Professor Hamway's."

"I'm not going to pressure you to talk about things that you don't want to disclose." Damen must have noticed my discomfort. He didn't seem pleased but also didn't press. Thankfully. "Seeing spirits and communicating with them is something else—a clairvoyant medium. Did you see something at Professor Hamway's house?"

I nodded, overwhelmed. "I saw a little girl early this morning. But I couldn't tell what she was wearing, or very much about her appearance. She didn't talk to me. And I couldn't pinpoint when she might have died…"

My recollection trailed, and a thought pulled at my consciousness. I could tell Damen; he knew more than I did about spirits. I'd originally believed I'd imagined it, but what if I hadn't? "I think there's more than one, but I'm not entirely sure. It's confusing, and I get a lot of conflicting information. It's hard to think."

Damen frowned as he wrote down something else. "We'll figure it out. Sometimes mediums can only see certain types of spirits. Good call on trying to pinpoint the year of death. You were at the library trying to research the house?"

"Yes," I admitted. "I wanted to search through old records. But I wasn't sure how—"

My statement was cut off as the double doors slammed open.

A disheveled Miles burst into the room. Without looking around, he began to pace in front of the fireplace, tugging at his scarf nervously. "Damen, this is a disaster! I haven't been able to find—"

He stopped as quickly as he began when he spotted me, and I couldn't help but hide behind my teacup under the weight of his full attention.

"You're here!" he said. Before I knew what was happening, he was already sitting beside me on the couch, his arm flung over my shoulders. "Did you get my note? Did you get the flowers? Titus wanted to give you chocolates, but I didn't think it'd be a good idea."

The statement made me blush even more. My stomach fluttered and I set my teacup down before I dropped it. "Thank you, I loved the flowers."

"Good." His face brightened. For some reason, me not running away made him happy. "In the language of flowers, hyacinths mean 'I'm sorry.' I thought it was fitting—considering."

I didn't know how my face could grow any warmer. However, my sudden anxiousness melted away as, after a moment, I was lost in Miles's chocolate brown eyes.

"I know," I heard myself saying. "I'm a botany major."

The second I said it, my heart turned to lead. That had sounded completely rude. He was only trying to be nice. I was a terrible person.

But Miles didn't seem to think so. His gaze softened and his mouth lifted slightly. "So you like plants too?"

"Too?" I repeated his statement. "Are you a science major?" I had never seen him around the department before, but the semester was still young.

"No, I'm in pre-law," he said. "My focus is on environmental law, though. Plants are a passion of mine."

I didn't know how it was possible for him to become even more attractive, but it had happened.

I wondered how he had become friends with Damen, especially since

Damen must be older if there was a grade difference between them. Titus, too. Julian, I could somewhat see the connection. Psychology and medicine were similar fields of study. But outside of that, it seemed like they all had such different interests.

"So did you agree? What did Damen tell you?" Miles asked, glancing toward Damen. "Are we going to have a slumber party after all?"

"Slumber party?" I asked, confused.

I had never been to a slumber party with anyone besides Finn. And while those were good memories, I had a feeling that this would be quite different—considering the circumstances and all.

Besides, wasn't it unprofessional for ghost hunters to refer to an investigation as a party? Not that I knew a lot about ghost hunters, but still.

I glanced at Damen, trying to see if he'd elaborate. He caught my confused look and smiled before he answered. "Absolutely. That's what friends do, after all."

"We're friends now?" Miles perked up, squeezing my shoulder. "Excellent! You did good, Damen."

I choked. I thought that despite our friendship status, Damen would maintain that they were supposed to be professionals.

But now that I thought about it, no one had actually said that they were ghost hunters at all. In fact, Finn had only said that his brother was *interested* in the paranormal; and Dr. Stephens had told me next to nothing before sending me to the planned meeting.

Oh no.

"Hold on." I tapped my chin, mentally going over the facts. "Are you guys ghost hunters?"

I hoped my imagination hadn't gotten away from me. That would be embarrassing. As it was, if they *weren't* paranormal investigators, then I was just a random girl who showed up at Damen's house one day.

"Not *technically*." Damen leaned back, and he and Miles exchanged a look. "We don't take clients or go around to houses with haunting stories. But we know *about* the paranormal and many things related to those topics. In fact, you could call us experts in the field."

Experts? What the fudge did that mean?

I was such an idiot. It was all I could do not to bury my face in my hands in shame. "Why didn't you say so from the beginning? I thought you were ghost hunters! I can't believe this…"

"Don't worry. We'll still help you." Miles rubbed my back. "Plus, it's not every day that a girl shows up at Damen's house looking for help. Don't feel bad. Dr. Stephens sent you to us because of our personal experiences. We're *like* ghost hunters. Did you…" He trailed off, looking at Damen.

"We were discussing that before you arrived," Damen responded. "Bianca can feel the presence of a spirit and can even see them to a certain extent. I'm sure there's more. She said it's been changing. We can look into it, but that's Julian's field. That being said, Bianca…" He glanced at me. "In cases like this, spirits are drawn to those who have these abilities. Have you ev—"

My phone rang.

Crap, bad timing. I snatched my purse off of the floor and dug around inside. "Sorry," I apologized as I pulled out my device. "I have to take this."

There was only one person it could be, because my parents never called me. Leaving the room wasn't an option. If I didn't answer right away, it would be worse.

I didn't even see their reactions as I answered the phone—hoping that they would just stay quiet while I derailed this train.

"Hello," I greeted pleasantly.

"Bianca." Finn sounded upset. Finn rarely got *upset*. He was mostly cool, blunt, and calculating. Immediately, my heart began to race as I feared that something terrible had happened.

"Where are you?" he asked.

"Um…" Why was he still looking for me? Normally he'd have given up and gone back to his books.

Whatever had happened, it must have been awful. My free hand gripped at my sweater as I feared for my parents, my sister, or…well. It had to be about one of them because I didn't know anyone else.

"What's wrong?" I breathed, frightened.

"You lied to me, that's what's wrong." Finn sounded furious. Even so, relief washed over me. No one had been hurt. He was only angry with *me*. That was the lesser of two evils.

Then his words processed, and my heart skipped a beat in terror. How in the world was I going to explain to him where I was? I barely even noticed Damen and Miles anymore. I had to fix this. "What—"

"Where are you?" he interrupted. I could hear the wind in the background—he was outside.

"Um…" Should I lie? That would be the safest thing to do. "I told you that I'd be at the greenhouses today…"

"Stop that. I'm here now, and you aren't," he snapped. "Where are you?"

I knew that lying was a terrible idea, "Um…" My frantic mind tried to come up with any excuse at all. A truth—a sorta truth? That might work. Something that didn't sound suspicious. "I'm at a friend's house."

"You don't have any friends," Finn replied. "And if you did, that means I don't know about them. And you don't know them, either. That's dangerous. You can't do that. What friend's house? Don't make me have to look for you, Bianca."

I frowned, somewhat disturbed despite my anxiety. What did he mean by that?

"Bianca," he sounded frantic. "This is your last chance. It would be in your best interest to answer me now before I find out the hard way. You've been acting suspicious lately, and I've had enough of it!"

Fear flooded through me—I had no idea what he meant by any of this. But *why* did he need to know where I was?

I couldn't tell him. If he was this upset about me being with a friend, who knew what he'd do if he knew said friend was his estranged brother. Plus, he'd connect the dots and figure out how I met Damen.

I was such an idiot. I never should have opened my mouth. This was all my fault.

My hands shook, and blackness swam along the edges of my vision. I had no idea what to do—what to say. But Finn was getting more furious by the second.

"Bianca!"

He'd find out. He'd find out everything and tell.

There was a sudden movement beside me. Miles had snatched my phone out of my hands and walked out of my reach as he began to pace in front of the fireplace again.

The world burst into color again, but remained hazy as I stared at Miles in disbelief. And now my day had gone from bad to worse.

They had to know it was Finn on the phone. Miles had been sitting next to me the whole time, and Finn had been talking very loudly...

"Hey, asshole. I didn't hear everything, but I heard enough. You can't talk to her like that! Who the hell do you think you are?" Miles snapped.

I jumped to my feet, desperate to put an end to this disaster.

But I hadn't taken two steps before Damen was upon me. He pulled me back into his chest, holding me against him. He tried to console me, making a shushing noise in my ear, but I didn't respond. My focus was on Miles, and my mind screamed that my world was about to come crashing down.

I could only see Miles's face—furious, as he yelled at Finn. I could no longer hear myself think as the nightmare unfolded.

Damen was shaking behind me, but I couldn't fathom why. I was grateful that he, at least, hadn't been the one who took my phone. I wondered if that was deliberate, because Finn would have recognized his brother's voice for sure.

"I don't care—you don't own her." Miles's voice sounded hard as he frowned into the phone. There was an indistinct sound of Finn responding, but Miles cut him off. "It doesn't matter who I am. All you need to know is that I'm her friend."

Another pause.

"I don't care why you think I sound familiar, but you can go fuck yourself."

With those words, Miles pulled the phone away from his ear and disconnected the call.

"Sometimes I hate that little douchebag," he growled.

My world exploded around me. "Finn is so angry…"

What was I going to do now?

Origins

Chapter Nine

Fear

Damen's hold briefly tightened before he let go, turning me to face him. His hands remained on my shoulders as a comforting presence. "Who cares, Bianca? What can he do to you anyway?"

While his words seemed harsh, his eyes were anything but. His gaze sought out mine—concerned and wanting answers. But I couldn't respond, because the answer to his question was 'a lot.' I had been so stupid. I never should have mentioned the haunting to Finn at all. It was my fault that it had come to this. I knew all along what might happen, but I had been so desperate I hadn't cared.

I had only hoped that Finn might have listened, for once.

Then I had picked a fight about my medication. Of course, he was suspicious.

Finn on the warpath meant he'd be seeking answers. And when he wanted something, he was relentless—destroying everything in his path in order to get it.

It was too late now. There was no way he wouldn't know that I had seen Damen. No way he wouldn't put two and two together.

No way that this wouldn't end with the same thing happening to me again...

"Bianca." Damen snapped his fingers in my face, causing me to jerk back and refocus my scattered thoughts. He frowned at me, his eyes blazing with anger. "*What* has he done in the past?"

I was stuck in a daze—numb. Cursing myself for my stupidity.

Indistinctly, I realized I'd taken a seat on the couch again. Damen was on his knees in front of me. From this position, my eyes were level with his face, and his arms surrounded me on either side. I could barely see Miles, but he was perched on the arm of Damen's chair.

Both of them wore concerned expressions. Why did they care so much? We had only just recently become friends.

Would Damen rescind his offer to help me if he knew?

I had not yet revealed everything—but both were watching me, waiting for me to tell them what was wrong. And I knew what they wanted. I had gotten them involved. Finn would blow this up, I was sure. They had to know—at least the history. It was only fair.

"I'm adopted," I began, my feelings fading into numbness. "I grew up in foster care until I was eight."

Damen shifted in front of me, and his hands rested on my knees now. Neither he nor Miles said anything, waiting for me to continue.

"I lived in three homes before I was adopted. The last two places were…strict. The couple in the first home taught me to hide the fact that I could sense, or see, things. Hiding my abilities became the only way for me to survive."

Damen started to say something, but I cut him off. I needed to get this out before I lost my nerve.

"When I was finally adopted, I started a new school. That's where I met Finn—he was in my class. Finn was always alone too, so I thought that I had found a kindred soul. I sensed he was being stalked by something malicious, and I couldn't ignore it. If I had, it would have killed him."

Damen seemed to be more contemplative than concerned. "Do you know what it was?" he asked.

I shook my head and glanced back at my hands. "I never saw anything like it before, but I also didn't know a lot either. It wasn't a human spirit though; I did know that. I had no idea what to do, so I tried talking to it. I told it to leave."

"I'm not sure what happened next, but it attacked me." I tried to be brave, as I recalled the dreadful events and the fear that threatened to make me puke. "I woke up in the hospital, and it was gone. Finn was there. The doctors said my heart had stopped and Finn found me. We became close friends after that.

"Not long after, it came back," I continued. "I was afraid to talk to it alone again, so I told Finn what I saw this time. At first, he was interested in what I had to say. So I told him more about me—about being able to see and feel the presence of spirits. At the end of the day, we went our separate ways, like normal.

"The next day—after homeroom started—I was called to the principal's office. Finn was there, so were my parents...and some strangers."

Damen's white-knuckled grip on my knees turned painful, and I squirmed. He released his grip with an apology. He abruptly stood up, the burning anger in his expression barely-contained as he glared into the fireplace.

"I can imagine what happened next," Miles interjected as he moved to sit on the coffee table in front of me. "And before you say anything else, I want you to know that Damen and I really *do* believe you. We *all* believe you. We've all felt that same loneliness in our lives. Please don't allow Finn's actions to cause you not to trust us." He took my hand in his, and his deep eyes only reflected genuine sincerity. "We will never abuse the trust that you place in us."

"I was diagnosed with acute schizophrenia," I admitted, staring at our entwined hands. "It was considered a serious case, and I was institutionalized. The only way for me to ever leave the facility was to admit that I was sick, to give in to their treatments. So I conceded and did what they wanted me to do. I didn't want to cause my adoptive parents any more stress or concern.

"But I wasn't sure about myself or what I had experienced." I bit my lip, wondering if it had been my imagination. "I felt deep down that Finn really did believe me that day. Something about the way that he responded—it was like he knew. I certainly wanted him to believe me. I was only trying to protect him. So afterward, when a blatant supernatural event happened again, I tried to bring it to his attention to get his reaction. But he would *usually* reason it away—or just remind me that I was sick. I never knew how he would react.

"In retrospect, I shouldn't have said anything to him this time, either." I let go of Miles's hand. "But I thought that if he came with me to my professor's home—if he heard the noises, then I thought he'd have to believe me. Rational people can't remain in denial about an obvious truth, right?"

The silence in the room was deafening. I glanced up, unable to miss the barely restrained fury in Miles's expression, and the blazing anger in Damen's eyes.

I was suddenly unsure of my confession. Why were they *this* angry?

Finn had only acted that way out of concern. Surely, they had to see that. He thought he was serving my best interests. After all, he didn't believe in the paranormal.

Right?

I attempted to alleviate the tension in the air. "It's not all that bad," I said. "You can't force someone to believe. He cares about me; that's why he gets concerned. His heart is in the right place."

Damen barked out a short laugh—the first sound that he had made in a while. "Seriously?"

The developing conclusion was undeniable, but that didn't make it any easier to comprehend.

"Damen?" I forced his name out, scared to hear the words that could shatter my world.

Miles cut off Damen's response. "Damen, not now."

Damen glowered at him, but it was too late. That was all the confirmation I needed.

I stared at my clenched fists. "It seems so obvious now. This 'paranormal experience' that you guys have is a family affair, isn't it? Finn *knows* it's all real, doesn't he? Are you *all* like me?"

I was surprised, however, when Damen let out a soft laugh at my question. "You really do come up with some wild, outlandish theories."

I blushed, embarrassed. After all, I thought I was onto something.

"But you are actually *somewhat* correct this time," he continued.

It took a moment for his words to process, my mind tired and muddled from the events of the day. Still, I didn't miss the proud gleam in his eyes as he watched me.

"Wait," I said. "Really? You're like me?"

"Not entirely correct," Damen responded. "You are two for one."

What was I wrong about, then?

"We have paranormal experiences because our families are involved with certain aspects of the supernatural world," he said. That explained nothing. "Finn, however, is fully aware of the realities of this world—paranormal included. But we are not sensitives." As he finished his statement, a dark look overtook his features.

I was in shock as it registered. He knew.

Finn *knew* that I wasn't lying—or sick. That the things I saw were real.

…And he still did those things to me.

The world shimmered, and even Damen wavered as my heart shattered into a million pieces. "Why would he do that?"

Miles slid to the side, and suddenly Damen was kneeling in front of me again. "I don't know why," he said, holding my hands. "But I'll be sure to find out."

"I thought he was my friend." I sounded so pathetic right now. "He was my *only* friend. I wasn't even allowed to talk to anyone else."

A storm brewed in Damen's eyes. "Like I said, I—we—will be sure to find out what's going on with Finn. He's a jerk, but he usually has a reason behind his actions. Probably not a *good* reason, but I'm sure there's justification in his mind."

Miles took a seat next to me again and leaned forward, catching my gaze. "It's not like he's been a very good friend to you, anyway. Based on just this one conversation, he's more like a jealous, abusive boyfriend."

I flinched. Yesterday, I would have been overjoyed to hear the word 'boyfriend' associated with Finn, but hearing 'jealous' and 'abusive' mixed with that label left everything tainted.

"I don't know what's normal," I admitted. "I thought he was just protective. That he really cared. I don't know what to think anymore."

"Normal is different for everyone. To find *your* normal though, you need to know what true friendship is like. There is a difference, however, between controlling and protective," Damen replied. "Luckily, you have us now. And we tend to keep each other in line."

There it was again. Despite everything, Damen seemed so sure that he wanted to be my friend. "I don't understand why you want to be my friend."

Damen's eyes lost some of that scorching anger at my question. "I'm glad you asked. Let me tell you a story."

I wasn't sure what a story had to do with anything, but I nodded anyway. He seemed to know what he was doing.

"Once upon a time, a handsome young man was waiting for his perpetually-late friend. It was the icing on top of a very bad day in a string of bad days. The young man had been bored with his life for a long time. He was full of ideas, but he lacked initiative and had no desire to do anything with them." Damen's eyes sparked playfully.

I fought the urge to hide my face, as I started to realize where this *story* was leading. Miles, on the other hand, didn't resist. He groaned and covered his eyes.

Damen continued, unashamed at how he sounded. "When his friend arrived—or so he thought—he opened the door to see an angel on the other side. He wasn't sure what to make of her at first. But when she said that she was friends with the devil, he couldn't help but be concerned. After all, no one could deal with evil without being burned. The last thing he wanted was for this beautiful girl to get hurt."

With every cheesy word, my face burned even more.

"Then he saw that she was loyal, brave, and imaginative. Something strange happened. For the first time in a long time, he felt inspired. He wanted to help her—to learn more about her." Damen paused a moment, and a thoughtful expression crossed his face. "Actually, it was more than a want. He felt as though he *needed* to be with her. Why, exactly, he wasn't sure himself."

He touched my hot face with his finger, lifting my chin until our gazes met. Despite the playfulness of his story, nothing in his eyes indicated anything less than complete sincerity.

"But there is something." His speech slowed as his gaze turned contemplative. "I can't place my finger on it, and it should be impossible. But there is definitely something."

Miles shifted, and I tore my gaze from Damen. Miles wore a strange look, and I wondered if Damen's flirting had made him uncomfortable.

I knew that *I* felt weird about it, in any case.

However, Miles only seemed confused—no hint of annoyance or embarrassment. "Me too," he said. "That's strange. It's familiar, but not."

I blinked at the two of them. What were they going on about?

Miles shook his head, then looked back to me. "We should exchange numbers. Since we are friends and everything."

"Oh." I glanced at my lap, ashamed again.

"It'll be more convenient to be able to contact you. And since you live on campus usually, you'll be seeing a lot of me," Miles grinned. "I might be a senior, but I live close to the library."

That was interesting. I'd figured that he lived here, with Damen.

He nodded knowingly. "It's too far to commute with my classes and study schedule. So it made more sense for me to have an apartment there. I do have a secondary room here at Damen's. Julian and Titus do as well, actually. In any case,"—Miles pulled out his phone—"you're stalling. What's your number? If you don't feel comfortable, you can—"

"That's not it." I didn't want him to get the wrong idea. But it was embarrassing… "This isn't exactly my phone…" I felt like such a loser. "It's Finn's phone. He has access to my calls and texts too. I know that he reads them, so he'd see…They said it's for security. I wasn't allowed to get a phone before he helped me."

You could have heard a pin drop in the following silence.

"I'm sorry," I continued to watch my fingers touching. "I've been trying to save up my own money—for living expenses next year and so that I could buy my own phone. But there's only certain kinds of work that I can do…"

"What do you mean by that?" Damen interjected. "Don't worry about the phone. But just in case…Miles, you turned it off. Right?"

Miles nodded, his face carefully blank.

Why would he have needed to shut off the phone? I didn't have a chance to ask before Damen stood up and returned to his spot by the fireplace. "You're eighteen, right? Your parents shouldn't need to give you permission to do anything."

"I don't have my driver's license. Also, I don't have a copy of my birth certificate or social security card. No one at the university office will give me a copy. They said it's against school policy. And my parents don't trust me with that information," I explained. "Brosnan isn't my given name.

94

Honestly, I don't know what it is, and I have no idea where to start looking."

Damen was scowling as he rubbed his temples. Miles wore a similar expression. He pulled out his phone and began typing without a word.

What was—

"Does Finn know that you have no identification?" Damen asked, his tone passive. "How did you even enroll in college? There's no way that they aren't involved then..." he muttered—probably not expecting me to hear that last part.

They were getting tired of me already. After all, this *was* pretty pathetic.

"Finn knows," I told him. "He said that it's normal to be protective of girls, especially considering my history. I know that the paperwork exists, but Finn and my parents took care of my enrollment here. I only had to choose a major."

Damen rubbed his hand down his face, and my heart clenched.

They were going to turn me away. I was too complicated.

Miles's phone vibrated. He checked it briefly before glancing up at Damen. "He says he's free for a late lunch."

Who was *he*? Instead of elaborating, Miles put away his phone and turned toward me. "Don't worry, we'll get to the bottom of this—and your ghost, too. In the meantime, if you can't use that phone to contact us, then we'll get you another."

"But..." Breath catching in my throat, I stared between the two of them. "You can't just—"

"Shush." Miles put a finger to my lips, silencing me. "I don't know if you've noticed or not, but—like Finn—we can afford it."

Yes, I might have suspected. It was obvious, despite the exterior of Damen's home. But I couldn't help but feel like a burden.

"If it makes you feel better, we'll put you to work. That way you can earn your phone," he stated, the corners of his mouth upturning slightly. "You can help me carry equipment and assist Titus with set-up and monitoring."

Titus—the mafia lumberjack? He was the *techie*? I thought that security guys were supposed to be brainless muscle.

Though, he was terrifying, hot muscle. But still…

Plus, that meant I'd have to hang around him. My heart thudded from trepidation. It was unlikely, but I still couldn't get over my unexplainable terror of being eaten alive.

Then something else occurred to me, and I turned to Damen in shock. "You actually have ghost-hunting equipment?"

Chapter Ten

Element

I glanced around the dimly lit restaurant. The crystal chandeliers hanging from the ceiling, inlaid gold on the walls, and luxurious linen on the tables—everything drew my gaze. After all, there was nothing else for me to do, since the three of us were waiting for the fourth in our party to arrive.

The atmosphere made me nervous, but Miles and Damen appeared to be perfectly at ease, as if they came here all the time.

And they probably did.

Miles sat next to me—our backs to the entrance—and Damen took the open seat across from him. I was still trying to come to terms with being a guest in such an elegant place.

When we first arrived, I protested, saying it was too expensive. I felt out of place and wasn't dressed appropriately. But Damen brushed off my concerns, stating that he'd add the meal to my tab. I had a feeling that my debt to them would grow alarmingly at this rate, and I suspected that they would not be keeping an accurate accounting going forward. I would have to find a way to keep track myself. I'd have to start off fairly high from the onset. No matter what I ordered from this restaurant, my meal was going to be extremely pricy.

My focus drifted. There were a number of open tables in the spacious dining area. So we weren't crowded. However, even with only a few patrons nearby, being around others made my heart pound.

Unlike me, Damen was the picture of sophistication. The shirt he wore under his opened jacket visibly stretched over his chest as he lounged in his seat. His legs were crossed, and—for the first time—I noticed a gold chain around his neck. There was a charm on the end, but I couldn't make out the symbol on it.

As we waited for our fourth, Damen browsed the menu as he sipped on some hard-to-pronounce wine—even though it was only mid-afternoon.

Occasionally, he'd glance up and grin at me, causing me to blush every time. Other than that, his main focus was entirely on the menu. Which was weird, because if he had been here before, why was he studying it so intensely?

Miles, in the meantime, was a picture of rugged sexiness beside me. He managed to remain mannerly even as he savagely ripped a breadstick in half and savored it with almost too much enthusiasm to be polite. It appeared as though Miles's weakness was food—something I mentally filed away for later.

They both avoided conversation and refused to tell me who we were meeting. Because of their actions, I had a sneaking suspicion who our lunch-date might be.

I brazenly stared at Damen—hoping that the power of my gaze would make him talk. In response, however, he merely glanced up and winked again.

"Would you like to try some, baby girl?" He held out his half-empty wine glass in my direction.

My spine straightened as I reddened in disbelief. And there was something else that I didn't quite know how to take.

He was offering me his *used* glass? That was *almost* like kissing!

"N- No, thanks…" I managed to choke out the words. "I can't drink. I'm not twenty-one yet."

"That's all right." Miles snatched the glass from Damen's hand and taking a sip. "I'm not either—not for another two months. Not bad. This would be better if it were a Riesling, but I can't complain," he stated matter-of-factly before finishing the entire glass in two huge gulps.

"That was rude." Damen frowned slightly as he glared at Miles. But he didn't appear to be surprised by his behavior.

I was shocked that Damen would permit underage drinking so overtly and in public view. Didn't he work for the police? How could he condone illegal activity? In fact, he was actually *encouraging* it! We could be arrested at any moment.

"I offered it to Bianca, not you," Damen chided Miles. "If you want wine that badly, order it yourself." He accepted his emptied glass with a sigh as Miles handed in back to him.

"I can't," Miles responded sadly as he tore apart another buttery breadstick.

Of course he couldn't! He was too young to order alcohol! He wasn't of age, and Damen was basically a cop.

I was a stickler for following the rules and would never dream of breaking the law. We could be imprisoned and kicked out of school for something like this. Our futures would be in shambles. Not only was I in big trouble with Finn, now I had this to worry about.

"My sister is working in the kitchen today. *You* might be able to do what you want, but you know full well that she thinks wine is only an evening drink." Miles sighed, staring at his breadstick with a look of longing. "She'd kill me if she saw me ordering some."

I had been sipping water as he spoke, and I ended up in a coughing fit at his words. Both men turned their attention toward me, concerned. Miles began to pat my back, trying to help me breathe while Damen uselessly held up a napkin in my face.

I shot Miles an incredulous look the second I caught my breath. "Seriously?"

Miles nodded, his expression grave. "Colette religiously holds to certain beliefs about proper food etiquette, like the way food and drinks should be paired. When it's her turn in the kitchen—"

"That's not what I meant!" I poked his chest, too horrified at the corruption of our youth to consider the repercussions of my actions—or to dwell on the serious pectoral hardness beneath my finger. "You shouldn't be ordering alcohol, anyway! You aren't old enough, and Damen is *practically* police!"

Damen raised an amused eyebrow, but didn't respond.

However, Miles smirked and leaned toward me—his brown eyes mischievous. "*J'ai vécu en France pendant trois ans.*"

I pulled back my hand in disbelief. Miles was now speaking to me in French? This entire situation was getting even more bizarre by the minute. "What did you say?"

"I lived in France with my mother from when I was twelve until I was fifteen." Miles grabbed my retreating hand and kissed my fingertip. "My sister grew up there as well. But she studied culinary arts in Italy before moving to America. She's the head chef here—this is her restaurant."

My eyes were large as I stared at him, and I distinctly heard Damen chuckle from across the table. Out of all the guys—even Titus—Miles was the one who had the stereotypical all-American look to him. I never would have thought he'd lived in a foreign country.

Besides, what did that have to do with anything?

I tried to get back on topic. "But that doesn't make it right. You're in *America* now. You can't legally drink until you're twenty-one."

"Relax." Miles released my hand and draped his arm over my shoulders. "The drinking ages here are such an American rule. It's not the end of the world. Who's going to tell?"

Could he be that naive? Visions of imprisonment and justice swarmed through my mind, and I couldn't talk. Instead, I pointed toward Damen with a shaking finger.

Damen shrugged nonchalantly as he accepted a refill from the sommelier, who apparently had heard enough of our conversation to find this all very funny. As the man left, I was left wondering what was wrong with these guys. Damen was involved with the police. Miles wanted to be a lawyer. This was a dis—

"Bianca, *relax*. It's not good for you to be so anxious all the time." Damen lifted his glass, swirling it gently. "There is absolutely nothing to get upset about."

Miles pulled me close, trying to reassure me. "What are you worried about anyway? First of all, I won't be ineligible for the bar exam because I had a sip of wine."

I wanted to point out that he had actually downed half the glass, which was equivalent to a large rather large 'sip,' but Miles moved on before I found my voice. "And no one is going to tell anyway. Everyone here is…" He paused briefly as he seemed to consider his phrasing. "A friend."

A *friend*?

That certainly sounded suspicious. People weren't *friends* with establishments. Only super-rich, snobby people were like that. These guys were loaded, but I didn't think they were that influential.

I narrowed my eyes at him, about to call him out on his lies, when a familiar silky voice cut in to our conversation.

"Sorry I'm late." Titus's smooth baritone shot a shiver down my spine. A fraction of a second later he stepped into my view, unbuttoning the top of his shirt as he slid into the seat beside Damen. "I had to escape from Maria. She said I had other priorities this afternoon."

Damen nodded, as if that made perfect sense, and greeted Titus in return.

Meanwhile, panic rose inside me. Even though I'd suspected Titus was the missing guest, the fact that he was actually here was entirely different.

Titus. Lumberjack, Mafia Titus was *here*. And, why was he late exactly? Did he have mafia business to attend to first? He didn't appear to be covered in blood. And who was Maria—his girlfriend from a rival gang? That sounded so cliché.

I stared at him with mixed emotions, but Titus barely spared me a glance as he nodded in my direction and greeted Miles with a grin.

I wasn't sure if I should be relieved by his lack of attention or be offended he was basically ignoring me. I didn't like being ignored—that was the worst.

So, he was mad at me. I should apologize.

However, before I had a chance to make a fool of myself, the waitress returned— engaging Titus in small talk. So, he was a familiar face here too.

Titus's hands waved in the air gracefully as he spoke, and I couldn't tear my eyes from him. Today, his hair was half up with loose curls falling around his shoulders in a wave. He was clean shaven, unlike the first time I had seen him, which made the masculine angles of his face stand out more.

Instead of the plaid shirt, he wore a pinstriped suit. It only served to make him appear even more dangerous and refined. It was difficult to decide, though, which look worked better for him.

Either way, now that I didn't fear for my life, I could see why he'd been called by *Forbes*.

I felt inadequate beside the three of them.

Miles had a wholesome, boy-next-door vibe. He was devilishly handsome. Plus, he had spent his early teen years in France—so he had that romantic, foreign aspect going for him, too.

Damen was pure seduction, with eyes that burned through your soul and consumed you.

Meanwhile, Titus was irresistible—angelic with a dash of wildness.

Then there was me—a blob at my best. And at the moment, I was far from my best. I hadn't even brushed my hair this morning.

I did, however, have my Burberrys on—that put me closer to their level, at least a little. I loved good shoes. They were the one thing that people would have to pry out of my cold, dead hands. I didn't even care if Finn had gotten them for me. They were mine.

But even so—being unable to make my own way sucked. I would have to Google ways to earn quick money. Surely the internet could help. I had to pay them back and keep up. I had no other choice.

It took a moment for the silence to register. The waitress had left, and I still stared at Titus like an idiot. Miles was eating another breadstick while Damen swirled his wine thoughtfully. Titus ignored me as he frowned at his napkin—a petulant look on his face. No one seemed to want to break the silence.

Yes, I would have to apologize to Titus.

"Sorry about your face and balls," I blurted out—feeling so ashamed I'd have to say such words in my lifetime. "I hope they're okay now."

Miles choked, and Damen's hand jerked so sharply that a splash of wine stained the white tablecloth. It took Miles a moment to compose himself, but once he had, he and Damen stared at me with wide, shocked eyes.

But it was Titus who had the most extreme reaction. Instead of graciously accepting my apology, he stared at me as if I had said the most ridiculous thing he had ever heard in his life. Which was quite offensive, actually, because I was trying to make things right.

I shifted my focus to the table—I had screwed this up too much. It was one thing to work with a scary Titus who was going to seduce and kill me. But it was worse to work with an angry Titus who hated me. "I guess you're still mad…"

Titus burst into laughter, and after a moment Damen and Miles joined in enthusiastically. I frowned at my place setting. This was terrible. I was awful at making amends, and this was proof.

After a moment, the laughter finally died down, and Titus wiped his eyes with the napkin. "Why in the world would I be angry? I'm not angry."

I blinked at him, unsure. "But…You wouldn't talk to me when you sat down."

"Damen said that you seemed to be afraid of me." His gaze bored into mine. He ignored Damen's protest as he continued, "I was trying to make you feel comfortable."

I was still scared of him, something ingrained. I couldn't fathom why. But if the others thought he was fine, then surely he must be. However, his actions made no sense. "How does ignoring someone make them feel comfortable? That only makes you seem angrier."

Titus frowned slightly. "I wasn't angry. You thought I was angry? I was trying to be cool."

"Well, you failed." Damen's eyes were closed as he touched his head. "Did you bring it?"

Titus perked at the question and reached into his jacket, pulling out a small, glittery pink cell phone. "Of course! It's the latest and greatest. I even took the liberty of installing some apps, wallpapers, ringtones—"

"Why in the world would you do that?" Miles frowned, lowering his glass. "What if she doesn't like what you picked out?"

She? I eyed the bejeweled device. "Don't tell me that's for me."

Titus slid the phone toward me, shooting Miles a confident look. "She'll like it. I have a sixth sense about these things."

"Are you sure it has nothing to do with *you*?" Miles muttered.

I had no idea what Miles meant, but Titus's confidence was rather assuming. Who was I to argue? I was getting a pretty phone—and pink was my second favorite color.

I curiously picked up the device and activated it, gasping in surprise. Somehow, it seemed as though Titus had discovered one of my weaknesses.

I grinned at the black cartoon kitten wallpaper. "Kutsushita Nyanko!" I sounded pathetically happy. He had also installed some games and other cute things. Finn had never allowed me to put personal stuff on my phone—stating that it was only necessary for research, calling, and texts. "Thank you so much, Titus. I love it."

There was no response, and I glanced up to see the three of them watching me curiously. But I was too excited to care as I flipped through my contacts. Titus had already pre-loaded all of their information—including Julian's. And had assigned each of them a character photo.

"Why is Damen 'Beer-chan'?" I asked. It seemed like an odd choice for him to be represented by a drunk bear cartoon character. But then again, considering he was having wine before five o'clock, maybe it wasn't…

"You jerk!" Damen glowered at Titus, clearly offended. Something resembling another emotion outside of lazy flirtation and controlled anger crossed his face. His cheeks dusted as he pushed away his wine glass. "I don't even drink that much."

Titus ignored Damen. Instead, he stared at me as if the world began and ended in my eyes. It was almost creepy—but for the first time, I thought I could really be attracted to him as well.

"You know *San-x*?" he asked, his voice filled with wonder.

I had made an idiot of myself. I set the phone back on the table and pulled up my turtleneck, hiding my face. I wondered if it was possible to disappear before dying of embarrassment.

"Don't do that." Miles pulled my hands down from my sweater and lowered the neckline back to where it had been. His fingers brushed gently against my skin, and the contact caused me to blush even more. "It's all right to like cute things," he continued. "This situation works out like a charm—it gives Titus a reason to buy stuff without getting weird looks from the sales clerks. Spoiling you is the perfect excuse."

Origins

Chapter Eleven

Betrayal

I finished up my rounds in Professor Hamway's private conservatory before Julian was to arrive. The boys had dropped me off after lunch—stating they had things to finish before tonight's slumber party. They hadn't wanted me to be alone in the haunted house, but I figured nothing dire would happen in the middle of the afternoon.

Besides, I still had my house-sitting tasks to attend to. I had responsibilities and couldn't avoid the place forever.

There was also the fact that I needed to decompress. My social anxiety hadn't acted up nearly as much around the boys. I had been more embarrassed by their flirting than anything. But all of the socializing and attention exhausted me. Being surrounded by nature had a way of calming me. It always had.

When things became too much to handle when I was with my foster families, I usually hid outside. It was there—in my second foster home— where I met Sir. He had taught me the little that I knew about my abilities, and about the plants and wildlife in the surrounding woods.

The last foster home…the woods had become a refuge.

A chill shot up my spine—and not from a ghost this time. I refused to let my thoughts drift into *those* memories. I had enough to worry about at the moment.

It was half-past six, and the boys were due soon. While I was thankful for my solitude, I was also excited about the prospect of being able to hang out with my new friends.

They had everything planned. Apparently, Julian would bring take-out. Then we'd set up surveillance equipment in every room of the house—including two areas I hadn't explored: the attic and the basement.

There was enough time before they arrived to take a bath and freshen up.

I was humming a song—a nursery rhyme that was often in my head but I couldn't place—when the doorbell rang. I paused, in the middle of putting away the garden shears, surprised.

I should have had time…

The doorbell rang again, and I realized that I was just standing there, motionless. I shook myself out of my daze and trudged my way through the house until I reached the large, wooden door.

Relief flooded through me. "Julian!" I pulled the door open the whole way, confused. I hadn't expected any of them so early—had something happened?

He grinned at me sheepishly. "Hello, Bianca." He tugged at his navy blue scarf, and I realized that this must be as awkward for him as it was for me. "I think I might be early."

He sounded exhausted. There were heavy bags under his eyes; and with every second, they appeared to become more pronounced. His statement had ended with a yawn—which he had tried to cover, but failed. He noticed me watching him, and blushed. "Sorry, I'll leave if you aren't ready."

"No." I gestured him into the house. "It's completely all right." I stepped out of the way so he could enter. I was nervous—I'd be spending the next hour and a half alone with Julian. I was also slightly disappointed, because he hadn't brought the food and I had nothing prepared.

Julian sleepily muttered a thank you as he followed me into the living room and sat on one of the velvet couches. "Sorry again," he repeated as he inspected the English-styled room. "I was already in the area, and my job ended sooner than expected. So I thought I might as well come over."

I mumbled—again—that it was all right and also took a seat. I watched him, unsure what to do now. This wasn't my home—I couldn't raid the wine cellar and play hostess. Besides, I had no idea how old Julian was, so there was that. There was no food—he was supposed to have brought that with him. But he did look tired, so it was likely that he had forgotten.

Should I offer coffee, or just conversation? I had no idea how to socialize.

Then, something he had said struck me. "Job?" I asked. "You work and also go to medical school?"

"Something like that." Julian yawned again. At this rate, there was no way he'd be able to fully participate in our all-nighter.

"What do you do?" I was curious—and also mesmerized by the graceful length of his legs as he crossed his ankles while I spoke. "Leg modeling?"

Julian, who had been moving to lean back into the couch, stumbled sideways in his seat.

Meanwhile, I was mortified at my word vomit and covered my face with my hands. "Oh my goodness." I couldn't look at him. "I just thought that your legs are really nice and…"

What was I saying? Men didn't like being complimented on their appearance—especially, their *legs*. This was mortifying.

"I was just curious about your job," I finished lamely.

Julian chuckled, and I lowered my hands as he regained his composure. He was sitting up now, and had his elbows braced on his knees as he watched me. "You like my legs?"

"*No.*" I groaned. I could never take that statement back. "Could we pretend I never said anything?" I tried to change the subject. "You should rest. Are you tired? You might want to take a nap, since you're here early."

He paused, looking at the couch longingly. "I don't know," he said finally. "It would be rude to—"

"No," I protested, thankful for this diversion. "It's all right. That gives me time to finalize things around here before the others arrive. And you do look tired."

Julian studied the couch for another moment before he shot me a thankful look. "If it's not a bother to you. I shouldn't really sleep—I should be helping you."

"You'll be more helpful if you aren't falling asleep where you sit," I pointed out, walking toward the linen closet to pick out a throw. "I'll have a pot of coffee ready when you wake up."

He smiled thankfully and accepted one of the fuzzy blankets that I offered him. "Just for an hour, then wake me up."

I didn't intend on waking him at all, but agreed anyway.

I couldn't take a bath with Julian in the house. What if he woke up and needed me? I couldn't fail in my duty as hostess. So, I spent the next half an hour lounging in the kitchen, both trying to kill time and figure out dinner. I couldn't blame Julian for forgetting to get something, since he clearly had a full schedule and was now being roped into helping me with my ghost problem.

At the same time, I felt strange. Finn never would have done something like this for me. Yet, now I had these new friends who were treating me as if they'd known me for years. Was this what friendship was supposed to be like?

The only thing I knew for certain was that I had to make this the best slumber party/ghost hunting experience they have ever had. And one requirement to get this accomplished was pure unadulterated caffeine.

I finished prepping the coffee maker, my excitement outweighing nervousness. It had been a long time since Finn and I had our last sleepover...

And once again, my thoughts drifted back to Finn. It was inevitable, considering I had known him for over half my life.

Everything about this day felt surreal. Damen had asked me to be his friend, I had gone out to lunch in a fancy public place...and Titus. There was too much going on, and I was way too emotionally exhausted to think about everything that had happened today with Finn.

I had both of my cell phones out beside each other, and it was hard to miss them in plain view on the counter. Throughout the afternoon, they had been a constant reminder of a problem I needed to address. But now there was nothing distracting me—not even the things I needed to take care of around the house.

It was hard not to compare the two devices. Not only in appearance, but also in what they symbolized.

Titus had taken the time to pick out something he thought I'd like. That action spoke volumes—even he was trying to be a better friend than Finn had ever been. And it was ironic that Titus had been right on the mark. Plus, the fact he also enjoyed cute things only made him seem more human, and less scary.

My gaze drifted toward the phone Finn had given me. It was still off—I had tried not to touch it much. But I couldn't avoid it forever.

Pulling it to me, I sighed. It was past the time my mother would have messaged me, and I would need to respond. Other than that, I would either have many messages from Finn—or complete silence.

I didn't know which would be worse.

The phone had barely started up before two alerts chimed from the device. Two new messages.

My mother's message was brief—as usual. She only wanted to know how classes were going. I replied that I was studying for the evening. And I knew that would be it, there would be no other inquiries into my life.

The other message was from Finn.

Answer your damn phone.

I wasn't sure what he was talking about—I had no missed calls. Before I could attempt to compose a response, the phone began to ring.

Finn.

My heart raced as I stared at the cell. What in the world was with this timing? I couldn't ignore his call, though. Who knew what would happen if I dared?

"Hello?" My voice was weak, but I didn't care. I just needed this to be over.

"Come to the door," Finn said emotionlessly. There was a click as he disconnected just as abruptly.

I stared at my phone in disbelief; and outside of my panic, a sense of righteous fury began to swell inside. It was an unfamiliar feeling, but I latched on to it like a lifeline. Anything was better than the fear. Because I was scared of Finn's reaction, but still...

How *dare* he command me around like this.

I'd come to the door, of that I was certain. And I would be calm and mature about it, too. Someone had to be the adult between the two of us.

My mind was in a haze as I stomped through the house and swung the front door open. I was not surprised to see Finn there, looking completely unashamed—and impeccable. He was furious, but I met his gaze without flinching. If it surprised him, he didn't let it show.

He opened his mouth to speak—

"What are you doing here?" I pointed my shaking finger at him. "You...you *butthead!* I'm very angry with you."

Finn's eyes flashed dangerously, but I couldn't remember why I cared. All of my succinct, planned arguments were of no use at the sight of his arrogant face. How dare he be angry? He was the one who'd lied to me. He was the one who was wrong.

"Did you just call me a butthead?" His voice strained, and his temper appeared to be holding by a thread. "Who do you think you are talking to?" He stepped into the entryway, bringing himself only a few inches in front of me.

I glared at his larger, taller frame. I wouldn't be intimidated. "Who do you think *you* are talking to, Finn?" I threw the words back at him. He was so close I could feel the burning heat of his body. But instead of making me feel secure—like it would have before—I became more furious.

He had no right to be mad at me. I wanted to punch him in the face.

"You lied to me." I spat out the poisonous words.

"What are you talking about?" Finn's eyebrow twitched. "Who was that man on your phone? And why has your phone been off? Where did you go today?"

I was seething. "Why would you lie to me?" Somewhere in the back of my mind, I knew it was a bad idea to rile him, but at the moment all logic had fled. "You were my friend. How could you do that to me? I *hate* you." I pushed against his chest, needing him to leave. I didn't want to see his stupid face ever again.

Finn's temper snapped, flaring to life. His eyes went wild as he suddenly lunged forward and gripped my arm, shoving my back against the wall with a crash. I didn't even have time to blink in surprise as pain exploded through my arm and back and he was in front of me again—trapping me in between him and the wall.

Usually, his anger scared me, but the fact that he had gotten physical didn't penetrate the despair which had taken root in my mind. I only needed to understand—why would he have done those things?

"Why would you do that?" My heart broke all over again. Seeing him face-to-face made everything more real.

"What are you talking about? Why would I do *what* to you, Bianca?" Finn's hand was on my face, lightly touching the bruise I barely remembered getting now. There was a flicker of concern in his eyes as he spoke. "Are you taking your medication? You seem to be confused."

Reality slammed into me, and my heart lurched while my fury fled. "Stop asking that question." I twisted, trying to break free. But my actions only seemed to intensify his anger.

He pressed closer, and his grip was now painful on my chin. My arm throbbed from where he had thrown me, and it was now being twisted behind me painfully.

"I can't protect you if you lie to me." Finn didn't seem to notice that he was hurting me—or maybe he didn't care. His hold tightened as he forced my head back, so there was no way I could miss the blazing inferno in his eyes. "Where did you go today, *exactly*?"

The power in his voice shot a chill of terror through me. I had never heard him sound like this before. He was terrifying.

I had been stupid. I'd pissed off Finn and made him lose his temper. Now I was trapped with no way to fight back.

"Let go." I tried to hide my panic. "Please, you're hurting me."

"Who was that man?" He didn't budge. I thought he hadn't heard me. "You aren't supposed to talk to people! It's not safe."

"No." My breathing was quick and shallow. I was on the verge of a panic attack. How had I never noticed his cruelty before?

"It's all right. You're sick, Bianca." Finn let go of my face. His finger traced my jaw—gentle, despite his words. "Don't worry. It's my job to take care of you. Just tell me what happened, and I'll fix it. Who did you see?"

"It was no one. Just a friend." I tried to move again. To knee him, or do anything at all in an attempt to get away.

However, he felt my movement and pressed in closer. The act caused a stab of agony to shoot through my almost-dislocated shoulder.

114

"Please let go." My plea fell on deaf ears. Finn's gentle touch turned hard again. This time, his hand gripped my throat. My pulse echoed in my ears.

I had imagined us holding hands, or hugging, for such a long time. I had yearned for his affection. But he wasn't that kind of person. Now he was touching me, but not in a way I could have imagined.

I had only seen this look in his eyes once before. It was as if he missed seeing me entirely. "Bianca, I'm going to ask you one last time. Who did you—"

I was released the same instant Finn's sentence was abruptly cut off, but I was unable to hold my own weight at my sudden freedom. Julian stood beside me before I could fall. His gentle arms wrapped around my waist. Once I regained my balance, he positioned me behind him. Putting his own body between Finn and me.

In the brief instant our gazes met, Julian's eyes were soft. However, when he turned toward Finn, his demeanor was anything but.

Finn staggered to his feet—he had been thrown into a thin table, and it had broken to pieces on the floor around him. That was the least of my concerns, even though I knew that I'd have to replace it. I was still in shock—staring at Finn back from behind Julian's arm.

Finn's blond hair was in disarray, and he jerkily readjusted his glasses. Blood dripped from the corner of his mouth, and I couldn't help but to follow the line it made as it began to stain his shirt.

Had Julian punched him? I hadn't even seen...

"What are you doing?" Julian's voice held a tremulous ferocity that had me shaking in fear. Or maybe I was shaking because I had been physically attacked? I wasn't sure...

Finn's eyes were hot with violence. "Julian!" He didn't even spare me a second glance as he glowered at the man in front of me. "What are you doing here?"

I could see Finn putting the pieces together in his mind, and could tell the exact second when everything clicked.

"It was Miles on the phone! I knew he sounded familiar." His focus shot toward me, and his glare held the promise of retribution. "Bianca, you went to see *Damen?*"

Chapter Twelve

Rush

I wanted to respond, but my heart froze at Finn's accusation.

We had already passed the point of no return, and I had never been good at confrontation. Earlier, I had foolishly feigned bravery with fury. Now, I felt none of that…

Past experience had taught me two ways to survive in such scenarios: strike first and escape, or pretend the problem didn't exist. Neither of which I could do at the moment.

However, Julian seemed to have everything under control.

"It's not your concern to know who Bianca spends her time with, or even what she does." He moved more fully in front of me.

I felt cowardly—and I knew I was weak—but at the moment, I didn't care. I could only force myself to breathe in Julian's calming scent as I tried not to hyperventilate.

"I wasn't talking to you," Finn snapped at Julian. "So stay out of this. This is between me and Bianca. She's my problem. You lot have your own responsibilities to deal with—mind your own business."

My body felt numb as I rested my head against Julian's back, stunned as Finn's words echoed in my mind.

His problem. He only saw me as a *problem.*

Julian tensed, but Finn wasn't done yet. "Why are you here anyway, Julian Kohler? Don't you have dead people to—"

"That's enough." Julian's words crashed over the room like a wave, and a feeling of intense fury saturated the air. "Bianca is a person—not a problem, responsibility, or your own personal toy. If you cared so much about her, you would have taken her seriously from the beginning."

"I have taken her seriously," Finn protested, his voice slightly more subdued.

But still, I couldn't look at him.

"I'm not sure what she's told you," Finn continued, regaining his confidence. "But she's ill. She's under a strict treatment regimen. Sometimes she makes up things for attention…"

My heartbeat sounded louder in my ears with every cruel word. Meanwhile, Julian's demeanor had almost turned glacial in its silent, deadly fury. He moved his hand back, barely touching my arm.

The touch was cold, but I wasn't sure who the chill was from at this moment. But then the contact broke, and he stepped away from me, moving toward Finn.

"You need to leave." Julian pointed toward the door.

Finn made a sound that was between a growl and a curse. "You can't tell me what to do, you—"

"*Now.*" Julian's voice brooked no argument.

I couldn't see what was happening—Julian had purposely kept himself between us—but less than a moment later, the sound of the door closing broke me from my stupor.

"Wait." I stared at Julian's back, disbelieving. "He actually left?"

"He had no choice." Julian turned toward me and stepped forward, running his hands over my arms clinically. "Are you hurt?"

I was staring at the wooden door, dazed, and almost missed his question. "What?"

"Let me help." Julian lightly touched my arm as he guided my shaking form toward the living room and to the couch. Pain suddenly broke through my shock. Even though he barely touched me, the ache radiated throughout my body.

He let go of my arm at once, moving his hands until they hovered over my shoulders. He seemed afraid to touch me again, and I almost missed the contact.

His concern, though, would have been more heartwarming if not for the situation. I only wanted to be alone—to lick my wounds in peace. This was not impressive, and I couldn't imagine what they had been thinking. I was so embarrassed that he had to see this—that he'd had to save me.

I was pathetic.

Besides, it was my fault, too. I had gone behind Finn's back. If I hadn't made him angry—

"Bianca." Julian's face swam in my vision. "Please, can I take a look?"

But why? If I let him do these things…if they continued to help me in these ways, I could easily become a burden and a "problem" for them now.

Julian seemed to sense my hesitation, and suddenly there was a touch under my chin, guiding my gaze up until our eyes connected. "Bianca, it's not your fault. You aren't a bother."

My breath caught—how did he know what I was thinking? And if it wasn't my fault, then why did fury still swim deep within those eyes of his?

"You're angry at me," I observed. I had screwed this up already.

He blinked in surprise before frowning. "Not at *you*." He moved his hand as he traced his fingers over my throbbing jaw. "I'm sorry you had to see that. I don't anger easily…" he trailed off before continuing. "When I saw what Finn was doing—heard what he was saying—it brought back memories."

More guilt swamped me—it wasn't hard to imagine what kind of memories. "I'm sorry."

"It's nothing you've done," he said—his hand leaving my face. "Bianca, will you let me take care of you, please? It's killing me to know that you're hurt. It isn't right. You deserve to have someone treat you kindly."

He hardly knew what I deserved, yet I couldn't hold back my tears. "I'm sorry," I repeated. "I don't want to be a burden."

I was so ashamed. This could have all been avoided.

"Don't cry..." Julian sounded lost. "Please, can I take care of you?"

I nodded. If it was this important to him, why would I deny him? Even if these guys didn't really know me yet, I knew I wouldn't be able to deny them anything at this point.

Julian paused, waiting, and it took me a second to realize he needed my sweater removed. I blushed, complying—thankful, I'd worn a tank-top. Moving was painful, so it took a long moment before I had struggled out of my sweater. I sat there with it bundled in my lap.

It was then that I noticed Julian had turned away while I was removing my clothing.

His consideration was cute and pulled me away from my dark thoughts. A med school student, and still so shy. I couldn't imagine why; I was probably the least intimidating patient he'd ever see.

But how to break the tension? I liked this gentlemanly side to him. "Okay..."

He turned around, blushing. But his expression fell once his gaze landed on me.

Well, that was disheartening.

I didn't know what I had been expecting—but not this. I didn't have the most impressive cleavage, or even a womanly shape. So I hadn't thought he'd fall down at my feet and worship me as some sort of sex goddess. But him paling in horror wasn't inspiring to my self-confidence.

"Julian?"

"Bianca." Julian closed the short distance between us, and his face contorted into a mask of professional concern. "Why didn't you say it was this bad?"

I had no idea what he was talking about. I hadn't looked at myself. And at the moment, I couldn't look away from him.

His fingers trailed over my arm for a moment, his gaze calculating, before he pulled out his phone and typed something. Once done, he put his phone away and refocused his attention back on me. "Where's the kitchen?"

Suddenly, he seemed like a completely different person.

"Oh." The question surprised me. I began to stand, intent on showing him the way. He pushed his hand against my chest, forcing me back into my seat.

"I'll be able to figure out what I need myself." His tone allowed no argument. "Just tell me which way to go, and I'll take it from there. You sit here and wait."

I blinked at him stupidly. It wasn't as if I was a fragile doll. But I pointed in the correct direction anyway—I didn't want another argument. He was gone at once, ordering me to not move as he retreated.

After he left, I looked at myself in the mirror to see what he was so concerned about. It was almost scary to wonder what might have a doctor-in-training looking so disturbed. Of course, he was probably overreacting.

Then I noticed the masses of bright red on the skin of my arm. It looked like a mixture of bruises and burns, but felt like neither. I didn't know how it happened, but it was jarring enough that spots began to dance in the corner of my vision.

Why wasn't I in pain? A memory stirred in the back of my mind, and I just knew I was dying. Perhaps I was in shock, or maybe my nerve endings had been destroyed. Should I go to the hospital...?

No, I'd rather not do that either.

My stomach lurched and I curled forward, trying not to be sick. It was both hot and cold at once. Something terrible was going to happen.

I was going to throw up. All that expensive, delicious Italian food. Those soft, wonderful breadsticks. The tiramisu. I'd eaten them for naught. I hadn't even drank any alcohol! Why was I being punished for being the responsible one?

"Bianca." Julian was back. "Bianca, it's all right." His hand was cool against my neck. Soothing. I opened my eyes—he was kneeling in front of me, various ice packs and towels piled at his side. "Damen is coming to help. He'll be here soon."

"Damen?" I could only look at him, confused. "I thought you were the one in medical school. To be a *doctor*. Damen is a psychologist."

"Psychologists can hold doctorates." His eyes drifted over my arm again. "But you are correct—I am in medical school. Technically, I could treat...this. But Damen has experience with this type of injury."

That didn't clear up a thing. "What kind of injury?"

He didn't answer as he helped me to lie on my back before packing in towels and ice-packs between my arm and the back of the couch. It was cold, and goosebumps erupted over my skin. It dawned on me that I was wearing a tank-top, and I prayed that my nipples would behave.

What a day not to wear a bra.

But he still hadn't answered my question. "Bruises?" I prompted.

"Yes, bruises." Julian didn't seem to be fixated on my chest, so perhaps I was safe. Instead, he focused completely on his task.

And he also didn't sound very convincing—I hadn't missed the slight pause before he said the word.

"But..."

"Go to sleep." Julian touched my face, brushing his finger against my cheek in a slight caress. "You need to rest. We'll figure out everything else in a bit."

He was making no sense, but I was too exhausted to argue. I hadn't really slept well the night before. Sleep sounded like a wonderful thing.

"Bianca." Damen's voice broke through my dreams, and a large hand brushed against my forehead. It was comforting—and really annoying at the same time.

There was nothing I hated more than being woken up.

"Go away," I mumbled, desperate to hang on to that last vestige of slumber. I had been having such a good dream. There were a lot of hot guys, I wasn't awkward, and I had been really thirsty…

"Bianca." It was Julian now. He sounded nearby, and a warm hand touched my shoulder. "You need to wake up now. Damen is here."

"No." Sure, I had said I would do anything for them. But this—this was crossing the line. "Tired."

I could sense their presence remained near me, hovering, and it would just not do. How would I be able to relax enough to sleep with attractive men looming about? What if I snored—or, worse yet, *drooled?*

I huffed, blindly grabbing at something that felt like a blanket. With my line of defense secured, I would just turn over and continue in my dreams. No one would bother me now—not with my face pressed against the cushions. My fortress was impenetrable.

Only, I wasn't in bed.

I screamed and landed face-first on the floor. I had also smacked Damen with my injured arm while falling, so said arm now throbbed in pain.

"Shit." Damen's voice sounded muffled.

I painfully forced myself on my hands and knees in time to see him tilt his head back—his hand flying to his bleeding nose.

Realization sunk in—I was two for four now. If I harmed Julian and Miles, then I would have gotten them all.

"Are you all right?" Julian knelt in front of me as he helped me to my feet and back onto the couch. "I'm sorry that we had to wake you, but we really need to look at your arm—"

"What about my nose?" Damen wheezed.

I stared at him—guilt racing though me. However, his flawless face wasn't lopsided—so it didn't seem like I'd broken anything. What a relief.

Julian waved him off, unconcerned, as he tucked the blanket around me. "You'll be fine," he said. "Stop being dramatic. You've survived worse than that."

"Damen." I was turning out to be a surprisingly violent person. I had never hurt anyone before, yet I beat up these handsome men. And, for some reason, they were putting up with it!

At least with Damen it hadn't been on purpose. "Damen, I'm so sorry. I didn't mean—"

"It's okay, baby girl. I'm tougher than I look." He expertly poked at his face—the bleeding had stopped already. But that still didn't make me feel any better. "We'll just know not to get in your face next time."

Next time?

My interest perked. Could he be planning on having many slumber parties? I thought this ghost hunting experience would be a one-time event. Weren't we too old for this?

But I couldn't stop my excitement at the idea. If they were serious about being friends, maybe we could make this a monthly tradition. I had so many things I wanted to do at parties, but Finn refused to humor me—Twister, Truth and Dare, Seven Minutes in Heaven, nail painting and hair braiding...

Well, we could do almost all of those things. Outside of me, the only person who could have their hair braided would be Titus. And I was afraid to touch his silky-looking locks. I didn't want to risk ruining them with my lackluster skills.

"That sounds fun. I'm so happy!" I smiled at them, so thrilled that they were contemplating a next time. It was going to be so much fun when we didn't have death looming over our heads. "I love slumber parties."

Damen and Julian blinked at me, surprised, before shooting each other curious looks.

Of course, that made me feel self-conscious again. I probably shouldn't have been so excited. Slumber parties were a normal thing that friends did, and now I made it sound all weird.

I lowered my eyes, frowning. "I mean, it sounds cool. Whatever you want to do."

"You want to have a slumber party, baby girl?"

I glanced up, wondering why Damen's voice sounded so very strange. His intense eyes captured my attention as he slowly brushed a strand of hair back from my face, and I nodded.

"Sure, we can have a slumber party. We'll make it a party to remember." Damen's mouth twisted into a breathtaking grin, and I wondered if he was being serious. "In fact, we can have as many slumber parties as you want."

"Why?" I hoped that my eagerness wasn't too obvious. "Because of the ghost?" That would make for a memorable party.

"Do you like pink?" Damen asked, his tone still weird.

I blinked at the strange question, my excitement slightly ebbing. What did that have to do with anything?

"And lace?" he continued.

My focus drifted to Julian, who stood nearby—his hand over his face.

I was hesitant now, and wary. Wondering what I might have said that would garner this kind of reaction. "Yes…" I answered slowly. "It's my second favorite color. Lace is pretty…"

He smiled, and it confounded me. I couldn't figure out why he'd be excited. Maybe he liked the color pink and lace in the same manner that Titus enjoyed cute things?

His thumb brushed over my lips, his fingers barely touching me. I gasped, and for some reason, that made his grin grow wider. "Do you—"

"Okay," Julian interrupted. "That's enough."

Damen pouted before his hand dropped and Julian continued, "Don't forget why I called you here, Damen."

That did the trick—Damen's weird mood vanished instantly. "Right." He rolled up his sleeves. "Let's take a look."

Chapter Thirteen

Burn

"I need you to turn around please, Bianca," Damen commanded, his voice all seriousness.

I tore my gaze from his defined forearms and watched him critically. Because *really*. Despite Julian's vague—but glowing—recommendation, I had reservations about this. The fact remained that Damen was a *psychologist*. What would he know about my injuries?

Besides, where I was supposed to sit? I was perched on a high-backed couch.

Julian seemed to sense my dilemma, and gracefully slid onto the couch beside me.

"Sit on my lap—facing me." He gestured toward himself with a comforting smile. I choked, but he wasn't fazed. "Damen will need access to your back. They are there as well. I noticed when you turned on your side. We'll need to contain these burns."

"E-Excuse me?" He couldn't be serious. It didn't matter that his words were made in innocence. And they clearly were—the man had blushed when I removed my sweater.

But it made sense. I could do this—I would just pretend that we were playing Seven Minutes in Heaven. Granted, it would have made sense to go to the kitchen instead. I could have sat on a stool. There'd be better lighting...

But maybe I didn't have all the details.

"These abrasions need to be handled a certain way," Julian explained. "Once Damen begins treatment, it might hurt for a moment. I want to make sure you are secure. You can hold on to me—it might help."

The two of them continued to converse in low voices and appeared to know what they were doing. I nodded complacently, trying to keep up. They must have done this before. They were the experts. And treating burns was bound to be a painful exper—

"Wait," I squeaked. Julian and Damen snapped to attention at once, giving me their full focus. "Burns?"

Granted, I had thought that they resembled burns, but to hear Julian classify them as such was a different matter. None of this made sense. How could Finn, only by touching me, have caused me to burn?

So I *was* dying? They didn't seem very concerned. "I—"

Damen knelt in front of me, taking my hand into his own. "Don't panic; it's not what you think."

"It's not what I think?" I tugged my hand away and shoved my fist against my mouth, holding back my scream. "I don't even know what to think. You said that I'm *burned*. Is that why I'm not in agonizing pain? Am I going to die?"

"No, you aren't going to die. It's not that kind of a burn—I don't think." Damen placed his palms on my knees and gazed at me. "Please don't worry. What Finn did…It's rare, but it's an ability inherited from our family. He let go of his restraint. It's more like…" he paused, his brow furrowed, as he searched for the words.

"It's like a physical wound—but on your aura," Julian interjected. "Normally, you wouldn't see it. However, in theory, in severe cases such as yours—or when the recipient is sensitive to these things—it can also manifest physically. There wouldn't be any pain until it covers your whole body, which would happen if not treated. It's a curse that will consume you slowly. The only people who can stop it are those who cast it or someone stronger. I *can* do it, but it would be better if it was Damen."

"What caused Finn to do this?" Damen asked flatly. I had the distinct impression he cared about the answer more than he was letting on.

"Because he's an evil little punk, that's why," Julian snapped. "Why aren't you angry about this?"

"I am angry. And that's not what I meant." Damen sighed. "Generally, Finn's control is admirable. I wonder what he's been doing that would cause it to be so fragile. And also, this concerns me because it's not like her type are naturally susceptible to this."

"I made him do it," I admitted, looking at the ground shamefully. "I yelled at him. I was just so angry—about everything. I told him I hated him. He might not have done anything otherwise. It's my fau—"

Damen's finger was pressed against my mouth, cutting off my statement. "It's not your fault." A strange emotion stirred in the depths of his eyes. "I just wanted to know what he might have said beforehand. I'm trying to understand his angle. That's all. No matter what you might have said or done, he had *no* right to lay a hand on you."

"Bianca, I'm not sure what made you get upset with Finn," Julian interjected, his expression dark. "But I am sure that he deserved it. Don't feel guilty."

That's right. I forgot that Julian hadn't been there earlier. "I—"

"We'll talk later, baby girl." Damen got back to his feet. "I'd like to take care of this curse first, please."

I nodded. That sounded rather urgent. "Okay…"

I had to take off my shirt—the marks had spread to the middle of my back—and I was tucked intimately against Julian's chest, my legs bent on either side of his thighs. Thankfully, the fuzzy blanket preserved my modesty, but it still wasn't much of a barrier between Julian and myself.

If anyone were to come upon the scene, there would be raised eyebrows for sure. But thankfully, it was only Julian, Damen, myself, and an unknown number of ghosts in the house.

Total privacy.

At least I wasn't the only one embarrassed. Julian tried—but failed—to act nonchalant about this entire situation, but the darkening of his face was undeniable. It actually calmed me to know I wasn't the only one having a hard time.

But, eventually, my curiosity overcame my shyness as I heard Damen muttering behind me.

"What are you doing back there?" I couldn't hold my questions back anymore, and my filter fled in face of my nervousness. "How will you remove the curse? Am I still going to have bruises? Will it hurt?"

Julian's mouth lifted, but it was Damen who replied. He sounded angry now, and his hand hovered closely over my back. Not touching—but I could feel the heat of his hands close to my skin.

"It might hurt a little at first. I'll try to be gentle, but curse-breaking is difficult. If it does hurt, beat up Julian. After a moment, you'll begin to feel numb and tired—having your aura manipulated is draining. And this is slightly different than what I expected…" His hands never once pausing. "You will bruise on top of what you already have. The marks will add more to your collection. It looks like Finn really did a number…"

"Can I kill him?" Julian asked.

"Not now," Damen replied. "Now I need to focus. Bianca, I'm going to start."

I was about to ask him what that meant, but a jolt shot through me. Even though I clamped my teeth together, a pained sound escaped, and I tensed at the unfamiliar sensation.

Julian grasped my hands, entwining our fingers between our chests. "It's all right." I glanced up at him, meeting his comforting stare. Then, the pain dimmed, and my thoughts became muddled.

Which was probably a good thing, because the intimacy of this position was becoming harder to ignore with every second that passed. All I could focus on was the feeling of Julian's body under mine, and the soft touch of his breaths passing over my head.

The world was fuzzy, but I still noticed when Julian tensed.

"What is it? Is there something wrong?" he asked.

"We'll have to see," Damen replied, moving his hands over my shoulders. "Bianca." His voice was closer, and I fought the urge to open my eyes. "What do you know about your birth parents?"

Once again, I was in that semi-lucid state between sleep and wakefulness. Damen repeated my name, his tone more forceful, and my eyes popped open.

"What?" I jerked up, snapping out of that place of isolation. Pain resurfaced, and my head collided with Julian's chin with a loud crack.

I had broken his face.

"Oh my God!" I gasped in both pain and dismay. I only had one victim left! I would have to stay away from Miles forever. "I'm so, *so* sorry."

Julian hissed out a curse and gripped my arms, but didn't push me off his lap.

Damen chuckled, somehow finding this situation comical despite its seriousness. "I'm beginning to suspect that this is deliberate—or you are clumsy. In either case, I approve of this payback. Good job."

"It's not deliberate! I've never been accident prone before!" I whined through my fingers. This was *their* fault—they were getting into my personal space all the time. Plus, their looks were distracting, so I was always flustered.

"I'm actually super graceful," I protested. "I used to do ballet. I'm so sorry, Julian."

"It's all right." He grinned, but his pained expression made me feel worse. "I don't think my jaw is that fragile. I'll survive. Meanwhile, Damen had something to say to you."

Oh, that's right. I glanced back at him.

He was rooting through a worn leather bag he had placed on the coffee table. "Do you know anything about your birth parents?"

"No." I blushed. "Is something wrong?"

What if I had an alien aura and I had never noticed? How would one even know something like that? That would be the worst.

"No." He stood, holding a tiny jar in his hand. But my attention remained on his serious face. "I'm curious about your lineage. And I'm wondering why Finn would throw such a temper, and why you'd have that kind of reaction. We need to figure it out, because if it's you…"

His voice trailed off, and he glanced back at his hand. I didn't know him well, but I knew that he was angry.

For a moment, I was dumbstruck. On Finn, anger scared me. But with Damen, it didn't. Instead of being frightening, Damen appeared imposing and powerful.

And he was upset on my behalf.

"… or maybe it's not," he continued in a grave tone. "Maybe Finn's been dabbling in things he shouldn't. I need to look into this."

Damen shook his head, coming out of his contemplative mood. "It's gone, and nothing permanent was done. If it makes you feel any better, I don't think it was deliberate. The pattern was too erratic." He was clearly addressing Julian, because this was so over my head. "In the meantime, a soak will clear up any lingering traces and rebalance her. We could go to the hospital afterward for the bruis—"

"It's not an option. We need to go," Julian interjected. "We can't let him get away with this. If he won't help, and you won't, then I'm going to intervene. Damen, tell me you plan on doing something."

Damen's eyebrow twitched, but when he spoke, he sounded calm. "Finn isn't going to get away with anything. But Bianca's treatment is her choice. Plus, there's still the haunting here to deal with. We need to research—plan. Then we can deal with Finn. We need to find out what he's been up to all this time."

"Do you want to go to the hospital?" Damen lifted his gaze and met mine. It was hard to miss the anger—and guilt—in his gaze. "Do you want to press charges?"

It took a moment for their conversation—his question—to register. But when it did, I gasped and clutched the blanket against my chest. "No!"

I couldn't believe that they thought that option was valid.

"Bianca," Julian chided. "First of all, you are black and blue. You need to see a doctor and get something for your pain. Secondly, he assaulted you. He *hurt* you. You should press charges against him. You have every right to do so."

"No."

I knew that he was speaking from a place of concern—but still. "I can't go to the hospital. I hate them. You're enough of a doctor for me, and Tylenol works fine. It's not a big deal. Anyway, I couldn't press charges, even if I wanted to—which I don't."

"I'm not even going to get into some of those things you mentioned yet, Bianca. But why can't you press charges?" Julian sounded sad.

It made my heart ache, because the last thing I wanted to do was disappoint him. But he didn't understand.

I bit my lip so hard that I tasted blood, and goosebumps broke out all over my skin.

Damen moved behind me, leaning over my shoulder to more fully wrap the blanket around my frame. The action surprised me enough to make me look up, meeting his eyes.

I wasn't sure what he saw, but his face grew even more serious.

"She's scared," he told Julian. Damen already knew—had gotten to the bottom of the fear I had been trying to hide.

Chapter Fourteen

Run

How could he do that? How could they take one look at me and bring all my secret fears and hidden thoughts to the surface? All I wanted was to be normal, but Damen and his psychology mojo had a way of breaking through my barriers.

I couldn't be a normal friend.

Julian was calm again, and he rubbed my arm comfortingly. "Why are you scared, Bianca?" he asked. "Do you think Finn will hurt you again? I—we—wouldn't allow it. Now that we have an idea of what's been going on, there's no way he'd get close enough again."

I shook my head—that wasn't it—before glancing at Damen for help. Though it was reassuring to know they were so determined. But there was something else that worried me more than Finn using me as a way to release his anger.

"She's afraid that he will tell her parents," Damen answered Julian. He sat beside us and took one of my shaking hands into his own. "That they'll make her go back."

"Go back where?" Julian looked confused.

I wanted Julian to know—he deserved to be forewarned about things that might come up later. But I was too drained to go over everything again today. Plus, my body ached.

I just wanted to pretend that everything was okay, just for a little while.

"It's all right, baby girl," Damen responded, almost as if he knew my internal exhaustion. "If there's a bathtub here, I was going to order you to take a soak." He held up the bottle that he'd grabbed earlier. "Use this." He sounded all professional. "It'll make sure anything that might still be lingering...*isn't*. And it will help soothe the pain somewhat."

I tentatively accepted the bottle. "What do you mean? I thought you got everything...You said it was a curse, but what did Finn do exactly?" I was sure he was trying to comfort me, but that ominous statement had done the opposite. "Besides, I can't take a bath. I have to feed you guys, and put the coffee on. And stuff."

Damen and Julian glanced at each other before Damen gave me a resigned look. "I'll explain the nature of our abilities later. I promise. You *should* know. But first, you need to *not* be in pain. And dressed..."

His gaze drifted toward my chest at his last statement, and I realized that the modest covering had gotten rather low.

I squealed and jerked the blanket up.

"Will you stop doing that?" Julian chastised as he moved his thumb in a circular motion on my hip. He frowned at Damen. "Don't embarrass her. Must you always be so...lascivious? You know—"

"Whatever, Julian." Damen threw Julian an annoyed look. "I'll do what I want. Why don't you mind your own business?"

And now I felt sufficiently awkward. This was a topic that went way beyond me; and I wasn't sure I wanted to be a part of this argument.

"I'm sorry." I moved out of Julian's lap without incident—they could figure this out for themselves. The last thing that I wanted was to overstep my boundaries, and I wasn't sure how their dynamics worked. Or even what ours would be like. Finn never had any cutesy nicknames for me. And I never would have sat on his lap.

This was going to be a learning experience. Having more than one friend—

and all of them guys. The only way to make this friendship work was for them to see me as one of the boys.

I could totally do that.

I would.

…But how did a group of boys act?

I'd have to do some research.

"Bianca, wait—" Julian looked guilty, and I hated that I made him feel this way. I couldn't let him dwell on this. I would just have to act as if nothing happened.

"Sorry." I held up the jar as I stepped away from them. "I'm going to go bathe with this…stuff. It's going to be relaxing and great… I think." I tentatively shook the jar—eyeing the contents. The powder resembled a mixture of Epsom salt and something I couldn't place.

I shook it again, and Damen jumped—almost lunging for me.

I froze.

So, shaking the bottle was bad—I'd keep that in mind. "What's wrong with you?" I narrowed my eyes at him, suspicious now. "It's not going to explode in my face, is it? Or cause me to break out in warts?"

He actually had the nerve to look offended. "Baby girl, do you think that I'd give you something harmful?" Even as he asked the question, his focus remained on the bottle in my hand.

"I would hope not," I answered. "That would certainly set our friendship off on the wrong foot."

"Don't shake it." Damen grinned, looking back at me. "Just go put it in some warm water, and you'll be fine. Make sure you don't make it too hot—only lukewarm. And be sure to soak for at least twenty minutes."

Bossy, wasn't he?

I glanced at Julian. He had already gotten to his feet and was pointedly trying not to look curious. He seemed all right with letting Damen handle the instructions. But he probably also wanted some answers.

"Don't worry." Damen stepped closer to me, whispering in my ear, "If you want, I'll fill in Julian with what you told us earlier—Titus too. You don't have to talk about it again. In my opinion, they should know. To understand what Finn is capable of doing—and your parents. Is that all right?"

"I guess so." I sighed. I didn't have much of a choice—it wasn't as if I could stop him. But it was really a terrible story. "If you think it's important."

"Hey." Damen moved back slightly and gave me an even look—searching my face. I wasn't sure what he was looking for, but he must have found it because his mouth dipped before he continued. "It's not about what I want. It's what you are comfortable sharing. I'm only suggesting they know because they'd be able to be a better support system if they had the details. But even if they don't know, they wouldn't abandon you. We've already said that we're friends, right?"

My face heated—this whole concept was going to take some getting used to. Heck, it hadn't even been a day. I needed time to come to terms with everything. But again, Damen was clearly something supernatural himself. I wondered if the others were as well. So why *not* tell them? They might even understand—at least a little.

My eyes focused on Damen's necklace—the symbol still unreadable. "It's all right if they know. Honestly," I whispered, and it was true. It didn't stop the shame, but maybe this was something I needed to do in order to move forward.

"Do *you* want to tell them?"

My pulse spiked at the suggestion. I was a coward, and I was also sore and tired. I couldn't deal with anything else today. I didn't want to see their looks of pity when they knew. I was gambling on them being able to relate.

I shook my head—I didn't want to be here. If they didn't understand me— if they weren't able to relate—I just didn't want to know.

"It's all right if you don't want to tell them, baby girl." Damen nudged my chin up with his forefinger, and his eyes captured mine. "I'll take care of it for you. Just say the word, and you don't have to worry about it at all. There's nothing cowardly about relying on others to help you when you feel weak."

What was it about him—them—that had me yearning to trust? That made me want to have more out of life? It was almost as if I had finally found a place to belong—with them. It was strange, and way too sudden.

But still…

Slowly, I nodded. "Please."

I still felt like a loser, despite Damen's reassurances that this was okay. However, I attempted to follow his directions anyway.

Take a bath, he had said. *Relax.* I had lived with anxiety for so long that I wondered if my body would even know what to do in such a state.

I eyed the jar while I waited for the deep tub to fill, wondering what exactly the bottle held. Damen hadn't liked it when I shook the contents, so now I was afraid to move it much at all. He said he hadn't—but would he actually give me something that might explode?

If I died, I was going to haunt him!

The doorbell rang, and the telltale sound of footsteps reached my ears. I frowned, knowing it was probably Titus and Miles arriving. Soon, they would all know about my past.

I wondered how Damen would tell them, or maybe he'd already told Julian. Probably not, though. It made more sense to only tell the story once. On one hand, I wanted to know how Damen was going to handle this issue. On the other, it was for the best that I didn't. I was sure to overanalyze any kind of reaction.

Besides, it didn't matter. Damen had ordered me to *relax*.

I turned off the water—the tub almost entirely full—before I poured in Damen's weird concoction. The smell of lavender immediately overwhelmed my senses, and I watched as the powder dissolved into a shadowy foam.

Some of my tension fled once I recognized the scent—the likelihood of being killed by a lavender bath was nil. What in the world had he been so worried about? Silly Damen. He must have been trying to scare me.

I soaked—as per Damen's instructions—long after the twenty minutes had come and gone.

I wanted to give Damen time to go over…everything. And also give the boys a chance to either come to terms with it, or leave. But, come to think of it, I hadn't heard anything for a while—not talking, not the sound of a door closing, and not even the ticking of the grandfather clock in the hallway.

I had been dozing at this point, but my head jerked off of my folded arms in alarm.

There shouldn't be complete silence.

This was not a good sign.

I had to get out of here. Jumping out of the tub, I wrapped myself in one of the large towels as I rushed toward the bathroom door.

It was possible—but not likely—that this was all a part of my overactive imagination. Even so, there was a sense of foreboding in the air that couldn't be denied.

But agony radiated throughout my hand as I touched the freezing brass doorknob. I couldn't turn it—I could only cry out, stumbling backward as I cradled my hand against my chest.

I had screamed—yet there was no sound.

I tried to shout again, to yell for help. But there was nothing—no noise at all. Terror raced through me. What was happening? Maybe Damen's bath mixture hadn't worked and I was dying now—or something?

The atmosphere began to grow heavy with darkness, and my panic thickened with it. There was something evil taking over this space. *Pure evil.* I had never felt anything like it before. The closest comparison would have been the sensation that caused the spirit last night to flee.

And now, in typical fashion, it was here—locked in a bathroom with me.

Origins

Chapter Fifteen

Voice

My breaths came in short bursts—and the air frosted in front of me with every exhale. It was so cold. So terrifying...

So dark.

I couldn't see anything, not even my own hands.

"What do you want?" I tried to say. But still, there was a silence so profound that I feared I would never be able to hear anything ever again. Terror didn't have a chance to consume me, though, before a sound—a noise that began so minutely I thought it was my imagination—began to come into focus.

Low laughter—feminine and sinister.

"Who's there?" I asked, and this time, my voice had returned. Although that wasn't much of a comfort, because now the only noises to be heard were myself and the unknown woman's cackling. My shaking hands clutched the towel like a lifeline as I desperately tried to see through the dark.

The baleful laughter grew louder and more grating with every second; and I didn't understand how—if any of the boys had stayed with me—they couldn't hear it.

Or maybe I was imagining this—I had fallen asleep.

I dismissed that thought the second it occurred. This was real—I knew it.

Just when I felt I might go crazy, the laughter stopped, leaving that dreadful silence in its wake. At this point, I didn't know which was worse. But at least I could hear myself: my heart pounding, my short gasps of panicked breath.

I needed to get out of here. If it hurt, it didn't matter. I had to leave.

Stumbling forward, I reached out for where I had known the door to be—but there was nothing. I had gone too far not to have run into it, or anything else. But it was as if all matter no longer existed outside of me, the presence, and this horrifying nightmare.

Moments that felt like an eternity must have passed. Every second, despair clawed its way deeper into my very being. I felt forgotten—unloved. I was a freak. No one even knew the depths of my despair. I would be alone forever.

I was being *hunted*.

No, this wasn't real.

I didn't know these guys very well—but something inside me screamed that this, connecting with the guys, was right. Somehow, I knew I could depend on Damen's offer of friendship. So, if that was the case, why was I feeling these things now?

Why was I huddling on the floor in a fetal position? This was extreme—even for me. I wasn't afraid of the dark anymore.

"I'm okay..." I forced myself up off of the floor. Whatever this was, it was very wrong. If I died now, for example, the boys would at least remember my name. Even if I would just be remembered as the strange girl Finn drove to them.

And at least Finn might remember me—for whatever reason.

"This isn't right," I reminded myself, trying desperately to think of anything I could do to escape this situation. If I stayed here much longer, I might go mad.

"Leave him alone!" a voice thundered from behind me—the volume so unexpected I fell back onto my knees and screamed. The presence that had been in the room since the beginning exploded in strength, and the woman's voice grew devastatingly stronger. "He's just curious!"

After those words, the presence vanished. But still, the velvet darkness surrounded me, and something different took the woman's place. I tried to scramble to my feet, but I couldn't move—frozen in fear.

But—physically—there was nothing here.

My face was wet with tears—I had never been more scared of anything in my life. "I'm sorry," I said, hoping to appease the angry spirit. I had done something to upset him, but maybe that would help.

He grew closer, but remained unseen. "*Mine*," his icy voice pierced through the darkness.

I was going to die.

My mind screamed at me to move—to fight. I had to do *something*. If I died, it might attack the others next. They'd never be able to defend themselves against something they couldn't see.

A feeling stirred within me—determination. I couldn't let this thing win. With a strength I didn't know I possessed, I finally got to my feet, despite the overwhelming pressure in the room. "What do you want?" There had to be something I could do—anything.

The air moved like a current against me—a feeling like silk against skin. And even though I was trying to be brave, I couldn't stop my whimpering as the sensation brushed down the length of my body in the dark. It reached my feet before it changed. A hand, the telltale sensation of skin, encircled my ankle, gripping me in a bruising hold.

I was lightheaded with fear, and the hold trailed up my calf, inch-by-inch. I screamed and kicked, moving backward as I tried to get away.

A current changed in the air, but that was the least of my concerns. There were other sounds now, but it was hard to hear anything outside of my panicked crying. A second later, the back of my legs smacked against the edge of the tub, causing me to lose my balance, and I tumbled into the now-glacial water.

The pressure around my leg vanished. And an otherworldly growl echoed through the room. "Tasty. *Mine!*"

"No." I huddled in the water—the freezing temperature a better option than the alternative.

The furious roar of the creature ended in a scream. Half-a-second later, I knew why. There was another presence here. A quick light flashing through the darkness, cutting through the evil like a knife. Driving it away.

An ear-splitting whistle had preceded the light, which left as quickly as it had come. But it had done something—changed the air. Had affected the evil in such a way that it fled in terror.

But what exactly had happened, I didn't know.

With the evil's retreat, the suffocating chill and darkness vanished. The dim light of the evening flooded the room, overwhelming my deprived senses. I was temporarily blinded as my eyes struggled to adjust.

"Bianca," multiple male voices called. And as the spots faded from my eyes, Julian and Titus had arrived at my side as they hovered over the tub. Someone's warm hands touched my arms. But I hardly felt it, or cared—my focus was currently torn between Damen and Miles.

Damen wasn't looking at me at all.

He stood some feet away, wearing a murderous expression. I was grateful it wasn't directed toward me but was focused instead on some sort of bird...thing. He reached out toward it, and as it landed on his arm, I realized it, too, was a spirit.

I had assumed, by some of the things I had seen, that animals had souls. But it was very rare to see the ghost of one. But I hadn't known Damen could see spirits, and the fact that he was conversing with the animal was very odd.

Miles, on the other hand, leaned heavily against the doorway. He was out of breath and looked pale and sweaty. He watched Damen with a somber look of his own.

What in the world is going on?

Within the span of a blink, the animal vanished. And all that remained was Damen and Miles—exchanging a look between them.

"Wha—" I wanted to ask what had happened, but my voice broke. The screaming had torn my throat raw.

"Wait a moment," Julian chided. He was kneeling next to me, watching my face. Titus towered behind him, arms crossed and stern. I probably should have been embarrassed at being wrapped in only a towel, but my mind still reeled over previous events.

Besides, there was nothing sexy about the current situation at all. As the shock receded, I felt like a human icicle. Every bruise and ache was back with a vengeance. Then there was my ankle…

It felt raw—bleeding. But the lack of blood in the water indicated that wasn't the case.

…and the water.

I couldn't find the door, or a wall, or even the sink. But the bathtub and water had remained. Did it have something to do with Damen's weird bath salts? I was certain if I hadn't fallen into the tub, then I'd have been in worse shape. For some reason, *it* had been unable to touch me in the water.

"She might be in shock. We need to get her downstairs." Julian's voice snapped me out of my stupor.

"No…" I tried to speak again, because I had only been thinking to myself. But my denial was lost in the shivers that overtook my body. I hadn't realized I was shaking…

I wanted to tell them everything was all right now. I could take care of myself. But I was exhausted and couldn't find the energy to move.

Julian didn't respond, but rubbed his hand down my arm before standing. "Titus, bring her," he said before rushing from the room. Titus took Julian's place; and for the first time, his large frame reassured rather than frightened me. I knew we would be around each other if we were supposed to be friends, but I had expected it to take longer to get used to him.

Perhaps I was shell shocked from the trauma, or maybe it was just hard to be scared of a fan of *kawaii*.

Titus gathered my body to his, arms under my shoulders and knees. His face twisted as he straightened. For a moment, I wondered if I was too heavy. But then he spoke. "I suppose you take warm baths, right? You aren't Russian?"

Was he…making a joke? Trying to make me feel better? That was kind of sweet. I shivered uncontrollably. I couldn't speak. I shook my head in response.

He frowned slightly before pulling me closer, holding me impossibly tight to his large chest. All I could hear was the steady, quick pounding of his heart. The warmth of his body was divine, and propriety fled as I molded myself against him.

He began walking, and his chest rumbled as he spoke. "She's freezing. We need to warm her. Who only keeps one towel in a bathroom?"

Fabric was suddenly draped over me, but I half-paid attention. The angles of Titus's jaw were distracting from this vantage point.

"Dude," Titus deadpanned, "you don't need to strip, Miles. We aren't *that* far away from the blankets."

"I am being a gentleman," Miles responded. I glanced down then, and noticed that Miles had taken off his shirt and tucked it around me. And now there was something *else* to distract me.

Miles didn't seem to notice my stare. "In my country, we are taught to treat a lady right."

"Stop using that as an excuse for everything!" Titus growled. "You didn't even grow up there during your formative years. I bet you spoke French to her, didn't you? You can't do things like that—speak English."

"Why can't I?" Miles shrugged, his muscles rippling as he strolled beside us while we descended the stairs. "You're only being protective because you didn't think of covering her first."

"I'm holding her!"

The conversation halted as we entered the living room. I was grateful for the interruption. While it had been fascinating to learn about my friends, and to witness their interactions, it was hard for me to focus at the moment.

The second we neared the fireplace, Julian approached us with a blanket.

I had expected Titus to position me on the floor—to let me bask in front of the fire. But without skipping a beat, he proceeded to sit cross-legged on the rug, cradling me as Julian tucked the blanket around the two of us.

No one seemed disturbed by this.

"T-Titus…" I shivered, even as the warmth of his body and the fire seemed to permeate my pores. "I can sit by myself."

He ignored me and spoke to Damen, who was now kneeling in front of the two of us. "It was freezing," Titus told him.

Damen frowned as he cupped my cheek, his gray eyes holding mine. He was concerned, but he also appeared to be angry. I wondered what role he—they— played in this. What did they know about what'd happened that I don't know?

His lips thinned as he responded to Titus, but he looked directly at me when he spoke. "It shouldn't have been affected—Miles made it. It saved her life, for sure." Damen addressed me now. "Did you use the whole bottle?"

I was struck-dumb by the intensity of his gaze—but still nodded in the affirmative.

And as my body slowly began to warm, another kind of warmth began to spread through me.

I was still completely naked—only the towel and shirt covering my modesty. The numbness befuddling my brain began to wear off, and it occurred to me just how closely I was plastered against Titus's body.

His plaid shirt was wet now too, and the thin layers between us left nothing to the imagination. I could feel *everything*. Every hard, defined line of his muscles. Every breath. I could hear every beat of his heart as it pumped frantically beneath my cheek.

It was hard to focus. What was with this man and plaid? How could someone look so sexy while wearing it? I didn't think the lumberjack look was a thing—until now.

What was wrong with me? If something didn't change soon, I was going to spontaneously combust. This was a disaster!

I couldn't see the rest of the room very well from our location, but I had to find the others. Anything to distract myself from him.

Damen had returned to his feet and paced between us and the fireplace. Meanwhile, Titus shifted to the side slightly, allowing me more of a view and helping the fire warm my back. Miles sat in an armchair, head in his hands. His shoulders were tense—and he was still bare chested.

And Julian. He sat on his knees beside me, whispering in my ear, "Give me the towel and shirt. And we need to switch blankets. Everything is wet now."

Titus must have heard—his heart lurched. I hadn't fared much better. My whole face was overcome with heat. What had I been mentally complaining about? *This* towel? It wasn't too thin at all. It was my favorite thing in the world—I never wanted it to leave me.

I glanced up at Titus's face, but his blank expression didn't match the pounding of his heart. I didn't understand why *he'd* be nervous, though. Unless, of course, he was scared of Maria. She could find out that he had touched another girl and would kick the crap out of him. Having a gangster girlfriend was probably frightening.

I was going to tell Julian that this was ridiculous. I could get dressed on my own—I only needed to go back to my room to get my clothes.

Which meant, of course, that I'd be alone. And right now, the very thought terrified me.

I was so pathetic.

Julian took my silence as acquiescence—because it really was. Thankfully though, they got no strip show. Titus maneuvered me around as if I weighed nothing, and Julian switched out the blankets and grabbed the wet items. I remained decent the entire time—which was a relief.

After the three of us settled, Miles finally looked up. He had been resting his head in his hands, and had been unmoved in his chair the whole time. However, the expression on his face was dangerous. I wondered what he had been thinking about.

"I'm going to *kill* him," he snarled—eyes following Damen's pacing form. "That thing was too powerful. No normal spirit would have affected the water. It had to be *him*. He's stupid, reckless, and childish. And I'm going to put an end to it."

Chapter Sixteen

Presence

"It's not like you to jump to conclusions." Damen stopped pacing and sighed wearily. "Or get angry. Besides, we don't know what *it* was—even though I do agree it was not something we'd typically come across in a haunting. But *normal* or not, it originated from this house. It couldn't have been him—although, it would be easier for us to assume so. We can't do that just because it's convenient."

"But look at what he did earlier." Julian gestured in my direction. "I told you that he isn't going to give up."

Oh. Realization slammed into me. They could only be talking about one person.

"It wasn't Finn." I forced the words out, hating saying his name. I was scared of him now, something I never imagined was possible. I felt terribly confused—lost. But that fear was a fact I couldn't deny.

Damen's focus shot to me, calculating. And the heavy weight of three sets of disbelieving eyes staring in my direction. It was obvious what *they* believed.

"I'm not saying that to defend him," I said softly, looking down at my feet on the floor. I needed them to understand. This had nothing to do with loyalty—or residual feelings that I might still have toward my childhood friend. "I'm angry too. But I've felt one of these spirits before. This is the third time. But it's never felt this intense."

"You've felt it before?" Damen watched me over his glasses. "And there was more than one?" He frowned, glancing toward Miles. "What about you?"

Miles paused contemplatively before he sighed and ran a tired hand down his face. "I don't know." He sounded resigned. "This isn't my expertise. I did feel something of a demonic nature, but you would be more aware of that than me. If there was something else, we missed it."

That didn't seem to please Damen at all. Titus and Julian were listening, but not contributing to the conversation. The scattered pieces of information were beginning to fit together.

"Wait," I interrupted.

At my utterance, everyone's attention drew toward me. I felt uncomfortable under the scrutiny, but continued nonetheless. "You're talking about more than ghosts, aren't you? Are you guys involved somehow? You've said you understand, and I've asked before—are you the same as me? Is that how you all know each other?"

I glanced at Julian, who was looking at me with wariness. "Can you all see spirits?" I pressed.

Miles's shoulders slumped and Damen sighed as he sat in another armchair. Meanwhile, Titus and Julian seemed troubled by my question. The atmosphere in the room went from furious to resigned in a matter of seconds.

My stomach twisted. Should I not have asked? Had I crossed some unforgivable line with the question? But wasn't sharing the details of your life normal amongst friends? I had, at least, told them some of my secrets. I understood about the fear of rejection—about not wanting to open yourself up to that kind of scrutiny. But whatever they had to say couldn't be any stranger than my background.

Then again, we had only just met. Maybe they were apprehensive about me too?

"Sorry." I bit my lip, looking away. I was ashamed I had even asked. "It's not important."

"No." Damen pinched the bridge of his nose. "This is new territory for us, to be honest. You can ask us *anything* you'd like. But I cannot promise to answer everything—at least right now."

"Oh." I glanced up. "So how do you know each other? You all seem really close, but very different."

"We've known each other forever and are a close-knit group," Damen replied in that same tone of voice. "Not a lot of people make it into our circle. Not that we don't have other associations, of course. But when it comes down to it, we are all we have. We don't even date—we can't. My family, as you know, is not normal. We all share similarities in that regard. That, and our roles within our families, keep us bonded together. We've never even felt the need to draw anyone else in…"

Even though this didn't make any sense to me, I could scarcely breathe. I was being trusted with the private history of other people. I'd never been so honored before in my life.

"…but there's something about you," Damen continued, his voice low as our gazes locked. "It's almost as if you are *supposed* to be with us. This feels right—and that doesn't happen. Not with us. That goes against our very nature. But we want to be your friends, and we want you near us. But I cannot tell you *everything* about what we do—not yet. That day will come as we explore this bond going forward. Is that acceptable? Or does this make you want to run away?"

"I won't run away!" I rushed to reassure him. My heart was fluttering with excitement. Normally, where fear and anxiety would have thrived, something unknown grew. I didn't understand it, but I felt it, too. The foundation on which I'd built my life had been shaken. I was in new territory now.

Whether or not that was a good thing, I had no idea. But I wanted to explore this strange instinctual camaraderie that I shared with these guys.

"It's all right if you can't tell me everything yet…" I didn't want to lie, but I *couldn't* tell them everything about myself either, for completely unrelated reasons. Some things had to move slowly, and I was perfectly okay with that. "I haven't told you everything about my past either," I admitted.

"But it's different for you, I think." Damen tilted his head, studying my face. "It's not that you don't want to talk about it, but that you can't. That isn't like our situation. This seems so unfair to you."

Freaking know-it-all psychologist.

I nodded in response, because he was right. There *were* many things in my past I should explore—revisit. But I couldn't put those memories into words, and the fear that accompanied those recollections was something I tried to avoid. It probably wasn't healthy, but I had no other choice.

"You deserve more than hidden truths, especially considering your reasons for secrecy. But regardless, I'm going to go for it anyway. What you do afterward with the knowledge is your choice, of course. You can ask us to leave and pretend you know nothing—but we'll still help you. All I ask is that you keep the secret." Damen sighed.

He crossed his arms as he sat back in his seat. "I've mentioned before that our families have expertise in the supernatural world. The four of us are from different family lines, and each family has their own specialty—so to speak. It's more complicated than it appears, which ties into details I cannot disclose yet. But I can simplify the situation.

"I am an onmyoji," he continued. "The Abernathy family members are known as experts in the spiritual and demonic realms."

My reeling thoughts slammed to a halt. His earnest expression made me feel like I should be impressed, but I had no idea what he was saying. This wasn't a simple explanation at all.

"Onm..." I tried to repeat the word, and failed. "What is that?"

The other three men focused on Damen, trepidation heavy in the air. Damen, despite being offended at my lack of awe, grinned at my question. "An onmyoji is a practitioner of onmyodo. It is an occult-based science that uses Taoism and other Chinese practices. Some onmyoji focus only on divination—which I can do. Others have other areas of practice—which I also do. But my foremost specialty is conjuring spirit-beings called shikigami."

I was still very confused. Finn had abilities, too—I knew from what happened earlier. But if this was a familial skill, did that mean that Finn was like Damen? Besides, that didn't answer the questions I had asked.

"So," I wondered, "can you can see ghosts? What is conjuring a spirit? What *kind* of spirit?"

"That's a topic by itself." Damen was still grinning, his expression lighthearted. He was probably pleased I hadn't run from the room screaming. "I can't see or feel the presence of what you'd call a 'ghost'. Which is, by definition, a peaceful spirit of the deceased. But that's a classification that exists only in a certain point of the process."

"A certain point?" I asked. "What does that mean?"

"When a person dies, one of four things can happen," Damen explained, touching the rim of his glasses. "They either head directly toward the afterlife, or they don't."

That made sense, but perhaps Damen was very bad at math. "That's two things," I pointed out.

He smirked. "If they *don't* move on, then there's three things that can happen—"

"But that's three sub-classifications within a parent category," I informed him. "So that's still two things—technically."

"Baby girl, hush." He rolled his eyes playfully.

I pursed my lips. The least he could do was get the facts straight...

"The earth-bound spirits," Damen continued, holding up a finger. "They are the spirits that sensitives and mediums would generally communicate with. They haunt the locations that were important to them in life. Generally, a house haunting is done by such a spirit. Usually they remain at these locations because they haven't accepted their death, or because they have some kind of unfinished business there. Sometimes they act out to get attention from the living. But normally they are content to haunt the spaces around them.

"Second," Damen held up a second finger, "are the most dangerous spirits. If a bad person dies, or someone dies burdened with negative emotions with no closure, then the negativity can warp their soul. Emotions are felt more strongly as spirits, and any earth-bound spirit is at risk if they remain seeped in negativity too long. The goodness they had—if they had any at all—eventually becomes overshadowed by evil. Their entire essence becomes demonic in nature. This is one way that demons are born, and they can reside either in this realm or in the underworld.

"And last…" Damen held up his third finger. "Are the unknowns."

I didn't like the sound of that. Granted, the bad spirits were scary enough, but at least you knew they were bad. "What's an unknown?"

"They are spirits who haven't realized they've died," Miles interjected. His arms were crossed as he watched the flickering flames of the fire. "Unless they become demonic, one of the strongest periods of a spirit's existence—when it's easiest to interact with the living—is after they've first formed. That is why you hear stories about families of the newly departed receiving signs from their deceased loved ones. Most spirits use that energy to move on afterward, and some settle to become earth-bound."

"People who haven't realized they've died," Damen continued, "are stronger by nature. Plus, they have the potential to do both good and evil. They have no awareness about what they are. It's a dangerous situation. They'll find out their true nature. It's inevitable. It's safest if they learn after they've weakened."

"But why?" That sounded wrong. I glanced between the two of them, certain I misheard. "You said that a spirit needs energy to move on. If they don't know they are dead until after that point, wouldn't they be stuck in that state—forever?"

"There are ways to help a spirit move on—certain types of people can help them. But they are rare. There's also exorcism, but that's rarely done. But if neither are options, then it's best that the spirit find out after it weakens," Miles replied, sounding remorseful. "Even the most mild-mannered people have the potential to react in unexpected ways. If you aren't careful, you could easily be facing a demonic force that could destroy you."

"That's scary." To say the least. There wasn't too much for me to say in response to this information overload. But some things were beginning to make sense now. "What's wrong with exorcism?" I didn't know much about what happened, but the way they said it…They made it seem like it was something terrible.

"People with my types of abilities exorcise spirits, but it's an unpleasant business." Damen glanced to the side. "It's something that is only done as a last resort. Outside of that, I normally cannot see a spirit unless it reaches a certain level. No spirit wants to risk being summoned by an onmyoji."

"How do you summon someone—with a Ouija board?" The idea didn't sound appealing to me. Generally, ghost horror stories began with a ceremony gone wrong, didn't they?

"It's different," he said. "When I summon a shikigami, it becomes bound to me. I can send it on tasks, missions—whatever I'd like. I can also make it fight against another spirit or demon. Of course, there's always a risk with owning a shikigami. They might not be willing to be yours. It is a practice that can backfire if the onmyoji is not careful."

"Wait!" I almost jumped out of Titus's arms as I realized the implications of what he had said. "The bird in the bathroom—was that one?"

I witnessed a battle and hadn't realized it? If I had known, I certainly would have paid more attention.

It was Damen's turn to look surprised. "The bird?" He and Miles exchanged a surprised look before he glanced back at me. "You could see it?"

Oh. I hoped it didn't upset him, but he didn't seem to like this at all. "I'm sorry…" I said. "I couldn't help it. It was right there and quite colorful. I'd have to have been blind not to notice."

The stunned expression lifted, and his mouth upturned once again. "The fact that you saw him means more than I can say. It also seals the fact that you belong with us."

Though I didn't understand a lot, at least this was the beginning of something. But I knew I had a lot to learn before I grasped the concept of Damen's abilities.

I glanced at Miles—and noticed he had been waiting to catch my gaze.

"I'm different than Damen," he responded to my unspoken question. Unlike before, he was nervous. "I'm not a medium, either. My abilities—my magics—are earth based. I have a slight sensitivity toward spirits. I can vaguely sense those that are tied to places on the earth, but it is not the source of my strength. I'm a witch. And witches focus on the physical happenings of our realm."

That was more surprising than Damen's revelation. I gaped at him. "But I thought women were witches and men were wizards?"

Miles rolled his eyes with a slight grimace. "That's a common misconception. Men and women can *both* be witches or wizards. But I'm only going to be a witch for a short time longer, anyway. I've been working my way up, but France delayed my education. I have a few weeks left. Graduation is October thirty-first."

I blinked at him. There were ranks? They *graduated?* I had no idea there was even an actual school for this type of thing—or that they were real. What was this, *Harry Potter?* "What level does a witch graduate to?"

Mischief sparkled in his eyes, and he gave me an expectant look. "I guess you'll have to wait and see, won't you?"

So they really did plan on keeping me around. My heart thundered furiously, and not from fear this time. It was pure adrenaline. Joy. We'd been friends for such a short time, and they were already sharing secrets and making plans for our future.

I wasn't sure how I'd ever be able to repay them.

I glanced at Julian, who was seated on the floor beside me. I couldn't keep the eagerness out of my voice as I directed my next question to him. "What about you, Julian?"

His face darkened at my question and he flinched. He didn't want to tell me. There was something—a deep hatred toward his abilities. I recognized it because it was the same expression I saw in the mirror every day.

I glanced toward Titus. He had a similar expression. It had slipped my attention before, but Titus was no longer a relaxed figure under me. His muscles were tense—as if he were fighting the urge to flee.

I recognized this for what it was—not a fear of me, but of the situation. A growing sense of kinship began to blossom toward both of them. I realized that Damen and Miles had come to terms with their capabilities, but Titus and Julian clearly had not.

It made me wonder even more about their supernatural powers, but I couldn't ask again. It would have been intrusive. All I knew was that they couldn't see human spirits. If they could, then Damen would have asked them about what happened in the bathroom.

Julian opened his mouth to respond to my question—despite not wanting to—but I cut him off. "It's all right, don't stress about it."

The words died, and his worried blue-eyed gaze met mine. And I didn't miss the glimmer of surprise within their depths.

"You don't have to tell me." I glanced between the two of them. "I'll trust you, and if we need to talk about it later, we can talk then. It's not a big deal to know right now."

Titus's muscles relaxed, and Julian's gaze softened. Julian leaned closer to me, and his finger traced along the curve of my jaw. "You are perfect," he said.

Julian's voice was so low I'd hardly heard him. But I did, and I couldn't stop the heat from rising at his words. He didn't seem to notice.

"I don't understand…" His voice trailed off as Titus interrupted, his velvety tones huskier than ever, "Just don't question it, Jules."

They both seemed relieved that I hadn't pressed the issue, and Miles and

Damen's concern faded. The tension in the room dissipated, and the four of them began to breathe easier.

In fact, if I wasn't imagining things, they all seemed relieved I didn't pressure them for more answers. It was as if they thought I'd be upset that they didn't tell me more.

All right, they could have elaborated a bit. That was true. But it didn't matter if they hadn't; I understood perfectly. They didn't need to explain another thing.

The group of them were paranormal, crime-fighting monks that had taken vows of celibacy. Of course.

That was why Julian had told Damen to stop flirting. That was why they couldn't have girlfriends. They had to maintain their innocence in order to do their jobs, and they kept each other in line. I wasn't certain how Maria came into the picture, but I was sure that had been misconstrued.

I could totally do this.

After all, with them being celibate, we'd never have to worry about silly love triangles. This entire situation made being friends with a bunch of cute, sexy boys so much easier. I only had to control my own raging hormones, but I would survive.

This was going to be easy as pie.

Chapter Seventeen

Requirement

Now that we had established the obvious—that the boys were paranormal monks—it brought up something else I had been neglecting: the fact that we were supposed to be hunting a ghost. There was simply no time to lounge around half naked—we had a job to do.

Damen and Miles seemed to agree. That is, if the low conversation that they were having in the corner of the room was any indication.

My fear and anxiety—ironically—began to recede the longer I was wrapped in Titus's arms. Yes, working with these guys seemed like a brilliant plan, now that I was dressed and had some more perspective. Besides, I now understood that Titus wasn't the only scary one. Damen was also kind of scary. Somehow, I felt much more at ease because I knew they were looking out for my best interests.

"Okay." I began to wiggle my way out of Titus's lap, trying not to grimace as the movements aggravated already sore muscles. "I need to get dressed into something decent. Then you guys need to put me to work—you promised."

Nothing escaped Julian's notice.

"Hold it." He sounded concerned. "We still need to get you something for your pain."

"It's nothing." I tried to brush off his concern. "I'll get over it."

Titus's hands remained awkwardly around my waist, giving me a steady rock to hold as I tried to keep my balance and not lose the blanket at the same time. "See, I can—"

"What in the world happened to your leg?" Julian's shock rang loud through the room. Damen and Miles stopped talking amongst themselves immediately, and once again, everyone's focus was on me.

I frowned, trying to ignore them. But when I let go of Titus's shoulder, my ankle buckled. A spasm of pain shot through my calf. Before I could react, I stumbled forward into Julian's outstretched arms.

"What the hell?" Titus was on his knees—I felt his unmistakable presence close against my back. "Are you all right?"

I couldn't respond. I couldn't move. All that ran through my mind—with my face pressed into Julian's chest—was that I hoped my butt was not exposed from this horrifying position.

"What is that on your leg?" Titus asked, angrily.

If my butt had been in his view, surely he would have said something. My heart began to calm slightly, and I found myself back in Titus's lap before I could regain my bearings. This time, though, my legs were outstretched and uncovered from mid-thigh down.

Thank God I shaved.

Damen and Miles were hovering behind us. Julian's skilled fingers deftly touched the area around my ankle and lower calf. He frowned and glanced away from the bright red strip of skin to meet my eyes. "When did you get this—from Finn? How did I not know…?"

I wasn't sure how he thought Finn could have hurt my ankle. But Julian did seem to have a grudge against him. Not that I didn't. I was hurt, betrayed, and furious with Finn beyond words. But this thing between Julian and Finn seemed to go much deeper.

"No, it wasn't him." I watched the way Julian's long fingers flickered over my sensitive skin. "It was that…*thing*. The one that Damen chased away."

Damen frowned. "But what did—"

"It—he—touched me before I fell into water," I confessed. "He grabbed my ankle and was moving...up."

"He?" Damen narrowed his eyes. "How do you know?"

"He spoke—they both did."

"What did they say?" Miles shivered slightly as he glanced at Damen. "I don't like this, Damen. To interact physically, even with a medium, takes a substantial amount of energy. Let alone to leave physical proof."

"We knew it could reach out physically—it already hurt her before. Now we're aware it is stronger than we thought," Damen said. "It won't happen again."

He then looked back toward me. "What did they say to you, Bianca?"

Shaking at the recollection and keeping my eyes trained on my clenched fists, I told them what had happened—how scared I had been, and the terrifying things that had been said. As I finished, there was silence.

Too much silence.

As I had talked, my hair had fallen over my face. Now I hesitantly looked up—unsure of what to expect.

Julian was sitting on his heels, and he, Damen, and Miles looked at each other. Titus, on the other hand, was barely breathing behind me. But his arms, which had previously been relaxed, were now as tense and hard as steel.

"She can't stay here," Julian said as he turned back to his previous task, which was examining my leg. "This is on another level, not just a haunting. I'm not even sure what's going on, but I've never seen a wound like this before from a spirit. It resembles a moderate to severe friction abrasion. I want to treat it as such. But if it's spiritual in nature, the treatment might not help. We might need to confer with Gregory."

Damen rubbed his chin and nodded. "I agree. But we'll watch it in the meantime. Dr. Stephens has a family emergency to attend to and is leaving tonight, so he'll be unreachable. He should have already turned off his cell, but he might not have left yet. Miles, can you let him know what's happening?"

"Hey…" They weren't going to try to make me leave, were they? That certainly wasn't the reason I told them what had happened. Besides that, I was the only one who could fully sense these things. And I had house-sitting responsibilities here—

"I can do that." Miles nodded. "I want to be away from here for as long as possible anyway. Once she's bandaged up, Bianca and I will drop by Dr. Stephens's place before we pick up dinner—Julian, you forgot again."

"I'm sorry." Julian sounded mildly chastised, but mostly annoyed. "I forgot again. But really, is food the most important thing at the moment?"

"Damen, don't you think she should go back to the dorms?" Titus rumbled behind me. "I did purchase all the equipment you requested. We shouldn't put her in any more danger. This isn't safe."

What did he mean he bought new equipment? They didn't seriously…

Outside of that, there was something more pressing. "No, I'm not going back to the dorms!"

The four of them froze before staring at me in surprise. They hadn't expected me to argue.

"Bianca." Damen frowned, speaking slowly. "I understand that you feel obligated, but this isn't your home. It's not your problem to solve. Why did you stay, anyway—after all this started? Why didn't you contact Hamway and just tell her that you couldn't house-sit anymore? Does she know about the paranormal activity?"

"No, I haven't spoken to her since she left. It's difficult to contact her, and also…I'm allowed to have friends here, anyway. Besides, the ghosts aren't all bad!" I argued—upset that they now wanted to send me away when I was the one who brought them here in the first place. "They aren't all bad. I can't just run away. I have to help her."

"Her? The one who trapped you in the bathroom?" Julian asked mildly. He was wrapping my foot with antiseptic and a thin, white bandage—the deep concern of his face masked over with determined professionalism.

"No, there's another girl too," I told him. "A child. If I can't help her, she'll be stuck—alone with those things. I feel it—I can't just leave."

"There's more than two? All haunting the same location?" Damen took a step back, shocked. But then his gaze turned stern again. "Either way, you don't need to stay here for that. And if necessary, we can observe activity from afar. But this isn't the first time it has attacked you now. You are still living, Bianca. You should aspire to keep it that way."

He paused for a moment, considering, before continuing. "Besides, this isn't the first spirit you've seen in your life. There's nothing that binds you to this ghost more than any other."

"I can't..." As much as I wanted to argue with him logically, there was nothing I could say. He was right. I couldn't recall the last time I was emotionally vested in the welfare of a spirit. It was more than wanting to become a stronger person. There was a pull—something I didn't understand—that made me *need* to help her.

"Is there something about this spirit that has caused you to seek out answers?"

"I don't know..." I didn't understand.

Why was Damen pressing me on this? Even if I wanted to leave now, I couldn't. At some point, I had become emotionally entangled, and I just had to see it to the end. "Everyone will give up and leave. It's happened before." Somehow, I knew that as a fact. "I don't even know...I don't know why we can't call Professor Hamway. All I know is that if I don't do anything, then nothing will change...She'll be trapped here forever."

I blinked out of my musings and held Damen's gaze. "*Please,* don't make me leave."

Damen had a blank look on his face, and the others were utterly still. He finally answered. "We don't abandon our problems once we've become aware of the situation. It makes no difference whether you are here, or safe in your room at the dorm. I'm not going to *make* you do anything. What I want to know from you is what is so different about this house—this ghost—in comparison to others in the past?"

I wished that I knew the answer. "I don't know…" I repeated.

I got the impression Damen wasn't thrilled. But I wasn't sure why he couldn't let go of the subject. If he was like Finn in any way, then perhaps he just needed to know—for his own understanding.

Well, more power to him. But I had no idea. So I couldn't help him clarify the situation.

I wasn't being difficult or evasive—I was just being *me*. Besides, it was my fault they were here. If they got harmed, then it would be on my conscience. "I'm sorry I can't be more helpful. When I asked for help, I didn't expect you to be in danger."

Titus's chest jerked as he scoffed, and I wondered why he reacted that way. His next statement answered my question. "I don't think it's *us* that's in danger."

I tilted my head back into his chest and looked at him. While I understood gangsters were fearless and tough, the spirits in this house had been other-worldly scary. A spectre of this magnitude could easily target any one of them…and that…well, that would be terrible. "You can't let it get you. You're vulnerable—you can't see them. I can help. If any of them come near, I'll warn you and you can run away. And we all need to stay in groups at all times."

Titus raised his left eyebrow higher with every word coming out of my mouth. By the end of my instructions, he had the most befuddled expression on his face—and I wasn't sure why. It was Miles's sudden laughter that broke through the pregnant pause which followed.

I glared at his shaking form. What in the world was he laughing about? This was dangerous business.

"Oh my God, she's freaking hilarious," Miles exclaimed, as he tried to regain his composure. I could feel Titus's chest heaving beneath me as he, too, found humor at my expense. "Asking her to join our group was the best decision we've ever made." Miles wiped at his eyes.

"I'm serious!" I narrowed my eyes at him.

Julian and Damen joined the two in uproarious laughter, and my blood pressure skyrocketed.

"Stop laughing!" I crossed my arms under the blanket as I pouted. I was only looking out for them, and they were *laughing* at me. See if I ever tried to protect them from harm again.

Damen nudged Julian aside and knelt down in front of me. I tried to ignore him, but when he stroked my hair, I couldn't pretend anymore. He waited until our eyes met before he spoke. "It's all right, baby girl. If we're going to stay here, then we'll *all* follow your rules—including you. No one—and that includes you—is to be alone in this house at any point until we've solved this case. But I think us guys will all be safe. I have a feeling this spirit is targeting only women. Even so, your concern about our welfare is touching."

Well, the fact that it was after women was a nice, sobering thought. But if it was so *touching* that I cared, why laugh at me?

"Thank you." An emotion—almost like appreciation—flashed across his expression. It happened so quickly I almost missed it. Damen's mouth turned up slightly as he continued. "It's not every day that someone actually cares if we can handle something or not or worries about our welfare. It's unexpected, but nice."

At his words, the amusement fled from the others as everyone exchanged some secret look that I couldn't decipher. Julian stated he was done treating my leg, and the exchange was soon forgotten.

Origins

Chapter Eighteen

Understanding

"Isn't it my job to help you with some of these? I thought that we were working on some kind of payment plan?" I asked, gesturing toward the large pile of electronics in the middle of the room. I was sitting at the bottom of the rickety basement stairs, watching Titus as he circled about the musty, dimly-lit space.

Julian and Titus had led me to the guest room so I could get dressed. My leg was sore, but I could have walked—painfully—if necessary. The only reason I had collapsed earlier was because I was caught off-guard. But they were taking no chances, and Julian insisted that I rest my leg for the night.

With classes beginning tomorrow—and Monday being my busiest day of the week—it made sense. It was hard for me to argue with logic. But dressing with two boys standing just outside the door was uncomfortable. I'd hurriedly threw on the first tank and pajama bottoms I could find.

After that though, I had refused to leave any of them alone in the house. Begrudgingly, they accepted my earnest pleas.

Damen—who had his shikigami to help if necessary—was setting up equipment in the upper level. Miles had taken Julian to visit Dr. Stephens and then pick up dinner. Meanwhile, I was assigned to 'man the base'. The job was only meant to distract me until the equipment had been distributed and set up—the *base* only consisted of a folded card table and a couple of monitors.

Titus had been tasked with handling the worst location—the basement.

Considering how much he had helped me, I felt obligated to see him through this deed. If the spirits overlooked his hulking, male frame and imposing muscles, it was possible that—with his long hair—a desperate ghost might mistake him for a woman.

Initially, he rolled his eyes and tried to leave me behind when I offered to help. But he clearly did not expect me to limp after him.

I won that small battle.

I still didn't feel I was being very helpful, though. Titus told me that keeping watch for rats and ghosts was plenty useful. So, I would do whatever I could.

"Your job is to sit on your beautiful behind and tell me if you see something." Titus gave me the directive as he assessed the situation. He was still circling the area, flashing a light into the dark corners of the room where the overhead light did not reach. "Besides, you wouldn't want to risk dropping our expensive camera equipment. Not when you can hardly walk. You *should* have stayed upstairs, but you are such a stubborn little thing."

"I can help," I protested. "I can hold stuff. Or hand you things. I wouldn't drop the camera." I grabbed on to the railing and began to pull myself up.

"Would you be willing to bet three thousand on that?" he asked mildly. "I don't think your nerves could take it."

I almost lost my grip and fell forward, but caught myself just in time. "*What?*" My eyes were glued to the pile Titus brought down earlier. "Did you go out and spend three *thousand* just on this?"

"Of course not." One of Titus's jean-clad legs moved into my vision, and my focus drifted upward along the length of his frame. He wasn't looking at me, though. He studied the room as he pulled his loose hair back into a ponytail.

For a moment, I forgot what we were talking about, but then he glanced back at me and pointed to one particular item in the mass of equipment.

"Only *that* camera cost that much. It's infrared—top of the line, of course. I'm not sure what everything else cost. I left the details up to Maria."

Maria *again*. The bitter sting of jealousy I held toward this mysterious, fluffy-haired blonde surprised me. Of course, I had no idea what she actually looked like. But a blonde would be his type.

Not that I cared *what* his type was. I didn't want to date a mafia lumberjack anyway. Besides, it didn't matter—since they didn't date and were celibate and all...

Even though I was desperately trying—*really* trying—I was still wary of Titus. Especially when we were alone. I wasn't sure why. There was something bizarre about him, but I just couldn't put my finger on it. Perhaps it had something to do with his dangerous presence, how large and terrifying he looked. Or maybe it was the sense of wildness and danger that lay dormant in his gaze. These were traits that the other three men lacked. But what better way to face your fears than open exposure?

If Titus was a paranormal-fighting mafia-based monk, then there was no way that Maria was a girlfriend from a rival gang. That would be unrealistic—who ever heard of a gang of monks? If one such thing existed, then they were all clearly on the same side.

She *could* be Titus's apprentice. I should ask, but it might give him the wrong impression. Like, jealous impressions. I couldn't ask—I shouldn't be jealous or curious. But maybe it was normal to know. Wouldn't it look strange for friends not to know this kind of stuff?

Then the words he had just said registered past my inner ponderings.

"Hold on." I put my hand up in shock, surprising Titus. He paused mid-motion, picking a camera up off of the floor. I continued before he could respond. "Are you saying that this pile of stuff cost more than three thousand dollars?"

He didn't move an inch but watched me—perplexed. Then his green-eyed gaze drifted to the pile for a moment before returning to me. This time his tone was wary as he answered. "Yes. I imagine so."

I was flabbergasted. "Why in the world would you spend that much money? All we need is holy water, and perhaps some incense. How long do I need to work to pay this back—?"

"You don't need to pay this back." Titus straightened. "My company collects all sorts of technology for research purposes. This is all a business expense."

I ignored him. "I'm paying this back. Don't argue."

My gaze was trapped on the pile now, it seemed to grow bigger the longer I stared. "I'm going to be working for free forever."

I should have asked for a written agreement. I had no idea what my salary was supposed to be in the first place. I'd bet they wouldn't bat an eye at paying me a hundred dollars an hour or some ridiculous sum of money. I couldn't let them do that. It wouldn't be right.

Such generosity was more than I could accept. I simply didn't deserve it. I just hoped they'd never be able to figure this out for themselves.

"What are you thinking about?" Titus asked.

I looked up quickly, drawing in a sharp breath. His face was now shockingly close to my own. It startled me, and—despite my best attempts—I couldn't suppress my reaction as I lurched backward.

Then I started to lose my balance and almost smacked my head against the stairs.

Titus quickly grabbed my shoulders to stabilize me.

I blinked, stunned, as I slowly came to realize what had just happened. Titus's body framed mine. One of his forearms pillowed my head—against the place where my skull would have smashed against the steps. The other arm was wrapped around my shoulders, holding me to him.

"Watch out." He sounded winded. His voice, along with the feel of his steady warmth over me, had my heart thundering in my chest.

"S-Sorry," I stammered. What should I do now? I could have seriously hurt him. At this point, I was capable of just about anything.

"Are you all right?" Titus shifted on top of me. And as he stood up, he pulled me up along with him as if I weighed nothing. Electricity ran down my spine as he held me back from him. His large hands were gentle on my arms. His gaze traveled the length of me—starting at my feet—surveying for injuries. Once our gazes met, he froze.

A tense moment passed before he frowned and dropped his hands from my arms. "You're afraid of me." Shame flooded his expression, and a self-reproachful look took over his features.

I hated I had been the cause.

He continued, his voice softer now—as if he were talking to a frightened animal. "I'm so sorry. I thought that it was okay…I've been picking you up and holding you all night. I just didn't realize…"

I couldn't bear the look in his eyes. But he kept on uttering apologies, not giving me a chance to respond. I wanted to deny he was right, but I couldn't. The fact remained even though it was different than yesterday: I was still wary of him. With the others around, it was different. But with the two of us alone, I couldn't entirely suppress the slight fear at the edge of my nerves. There was something dark about him, and I knew that he *could* hurt me without breaking a sweat.

Yes, any one of them could hurt me if they wanted to. But Titus was different.

Eventually, I would get over my fear. I knew that I could. But I would never be able to do so if I wasn't honest with him.

"Why?" he mused, frowning. "Is it because I didn't back off yesterday? Miles tells me that I'm pushy and overbearing. But I was only concerned about you, and you were walking alone—"

I couldn't take it anymore. He *had* been nice to me, even then. Pushy or not. And even though I had physically attacked him, he still welcomed me into the group without question. Even now, he *still* wanted to help me. He had gone out of his way, despite hardly knowing me.

He was a good person. I knew that, too. Scary, but good. I couldn't let him feel guilty about something that wasn't his fault.

"Stop." I pressed my fingers to his lips—standing on the stairs made the action easier. His stunned gaze locked with mine as his words trailed off. "It's not you," I told him. "I'm damaged. Quirky. I have very weird instincts. Outside of the initial creepiness, you did nothing wrong."

Titus blinked at me in confusion, his face relaxing. He seemed to have no idea how to respond.

He seemed clueless about certain social norms—not that I was an expert. But I was certain that most people didn't just show up at a girl's house after she kicked him in the balls.

Finally, he appeared to make up his mind. His voice was low as he asked, "What do you mean by damaged?"

During the silence, my focus had been captured by a loose curl. It had fallen seductively in front of his eyes, and I was entranced. But at his question, I realized what I had done—what I'd said.

How much I nearly gave away.

These guys seemed to do that to me. They had a knack for catching me off guard. It scared me—but also drew me in. I desperately sought the peace they offered—but not right now. Not until I figured out what this friendship meant and how our dynamics would play out.

I blinked and stepped back. Trying to nonchalantly brush off what I had said, I grinned. "Sorry. That's not what I meant." I didn't think he was fooled. Nevertheless, we weren't going down *that* road. Not now, anyway.

Besides, that had nothing to do with the current topic.

I had promised to be honest about my feelings. "I am scared of you. But it's not because of that."

Titus frowned, clearly displeased. I sensed that—by my words—I tainted something irreparable in our budding friendship. "Are you afraid of the others?" he asked. At the back-and-forth shake of my head, his frown deepened. A flicker of hurt flashed in his green eyes. "If it makes you feel better, I can leave—"

He started to walk past me, to go up the stairs. If I didn't stop him now, any hope of friendship between us would be shattered forever. Even if he was scary, I wanted to get know him. I couldn't be friends with the others and reject him.

And I also wanted to overcome this irrational fear.

My arm shot out before I could second guess myself, and I caught his wrist.

He was infinitely stronger than me, so he could have easily broken my hold and left me, severing our weak connection forever. However, as soon as he felt my touch, he froze. It was almost as though he didn't want it to end this way either.

"I'm sorry." I stared at my hand, noticing that I couldn't even span the circumference of his wrist. "I don't want you to go. I'll get over it. I don't mind talking to you—or the touching."

Titus pivoted in front of me, placing his hands back on my shoulders. He lightly moved his thumbs in comforting circles on my arms. But still, he didn't say a word.

I glanced up, and he raised his arm until one of his fingers trailed the side of my face and reached the lobe of my ear. He was watching me with the most indescribable expression, and I didn't understand at all.

Then he spoke, and there was an underlying thread of hope in his voice. "What can I do to ease your fears? What are you afraid of—exactly?"

My breath hitched. I couldn't believe it—he was trying to understand. To be accommodating. But I couldn't describe this irrational fear I was experiencing.

"I really don't know," I admitted. "For some reason, I'm afraid you'll hurt me. Your presence is overwhelming. I don't know how to take it. I feel like you could easily destroy me."

Understanding crossed his expression—which confused me because none of this made any sense. But then his face relaxed into a smile—that same seductive grin he wore when we'd first met.

Somehow, everything was going to be all right. That he knew what to do now. "Don't worry, beautiful." His finger caressed my cheek again before he stepped back. "The last thing in the world that I'd ever do would be destroy you. You'll always be safe with me."

Then he turned away and returned to the pile of electronics as if nothing had happened. In fact, he seemed to be in a much better mood at that point and even started whistling.

Meanwhile, I felt dazed. I returned to my seat at the bottom stair and watched him in confusion. Seeing him so open, so accepting, put me at ease in a way nothing else could have. In fact, his reaction sealed the fact that Titus was an inexplicably good person. Of course, my heart still pounded. I wished I understood what had just transpired.

Chapter Nineteen

Watch

"Here you go, beautiful." A half-hour later, Titus led me to the living room—his arm wrapped around my waist for support—toward one of two office chairs. Chairs that definitely had not been there before.

A laptop and monitors had also been arranged on top of the previously empty table. Damen had been busy, but the basement had taken longer to set up than originally anticipated. However, things were now beginning to resemble how I imagined a ghost-hunting base to look.

Titus gestured to one of the empty chairs. "Sit your pretty butt here," he commanded.

I obeyed.

He pushed my chair under the table and continued speaking as he took a seat of his own. "One of your jobs will be to watch these monitors. Even though we don't normally take on cases, we have done this before. But not with this type of advanced equipment. I'll help you get acclimated while we go over some of the new features together."

He brought my attention to the monitors, which showed multiple split-screens. I noticed that each split-screen had been labeled with a different section of the basement, one for every room in the house. Right now, there was nothing on the screens.

"We've installed regular and thermal cameras in each room," Titus said as he began to type.

The screens flickered to life, and instantly, a multitude of colors displayed within each box.

"This is the view of the rooms using thermal technology," Titus answered my unspoken question. "Using thermal recordings to see a spirit is not an exact technology. But if we find areas of intense cold, we can look into that location further. We also have a secondary monitoring system." Titus typed something else, and the screens changed. This time, the rooms appeared to be tinted green. "This view is from the night-vision cameras. We can alternate and record scenes between the two views as needed."

I nodded along as he spoke, finding this all to be fascinating.

"We have something even better though," Titus said, shooting me a glance.

"What's that?" I whispered back, awed. I couldn't believe they had done all of this. What could be better than all of this ridiculously expensive technology?

"You, of course." Titus suddenly looked shy. "You being here makes this job so much easier. A medium is always more sensitive than any type of technology. Nevertheless, we put these systems in place to enable us to record areas for physical proof. If this job is not completed before your professor returns, we will be able to provide her with evidence that there's a haunting at this house. Then we can finish the project."

I was stunned. They had never planned on leaving this uncompleted. They were going to see it through. I had been worried for nothing. "What do we do once we've seen the spirits?"

Titus frowned. "It depends."

"Depends on what?"

"What kind of spirit it is," Damen said as he strolled into the room, holding two cups of coffee.

He handed me one. The contents were light in color. I hadn't told him how I took my coffee... I glanced at Titus—was this his?

"I don't drink coffee," Titus said.

"It's light and sweet," Damen replied as he sat on the couch with a smirk on his face. "I assumed since you were drinking that fake coffee earlier in the library, and from the way that you prepared your tea, that you took your coffee the same way."

"A mocha latte isn't fake coffee…" My heart thundered as I argued my—admittedly weak—point. I sipped at the proffered mug, wondering why Damen would have paid that much attention to my drink when we'd went out. He wasn't interested in me. But then again, Damen seemed to want to know everything and never be wrong. It was probably a part of his nature. "Thank you."

Damen grinned, then a more serious expression took over. "To answer your question, if the spirits are 'evil,' which we know they are, and if we can locate them again, I might have to perform an exorcism. The other girl spirit? I am not sure. We need more answers. The most we might be able to do would be to make her more comfortable in her resting place. She might be having difficulties with more negative spirits around."

"But I thought you said that exorcisms were bad?"

"They are." Damen set his coffee aside and leaned forward, resting his elbows on his knees. "Only the truly evil deserve to be exorcised—and human souls are different than most. Humans, they can live forever in some manner or other. But to be exorcised removes all traces of their existence from both the natural and the spiritual realms. There are some debates on whether or not it's ethical to exorcise a human, or whether those who have become evil are redeemable or not."

"Oh…I didn't know that." Now I was glad that I hadn't looked up how to exorcise the spirit girl. I could have done something irreparable.

"Don't worry." Damen met my eyes. "That's why we're here. To help."

I started to speak, to thank him, when my phone vibrated, startling the three of us.

Both of my phones were at the other end of the table—Damen must have brought them in from the kitchen. The alert had come from one of them.

A surge of panic momentarily blinded me—was Finn calling me again? I was not ready to deal with him tonight, even though I knew things were far from over. But then I recalled that my first phone was rarely set on vibrate.

I reached out for the pink device, but Titus beat me to it—sliding it to me with a wink. Was it obvious my blood was rushing excitedly through me? But I couldn't help myself—which of my new friends had texted me, and why?

Julian: *What kind of Chinese food do you like?*

I tilted my head to the side curiously—bemused. How fitting that my first conversation on my new phone would be about food. Food was life, after all. However, in answer to that particular question…

Me: *I don't know. I've only ever had lo mein. But I don't want noodles. What do you recommend?*

He didn't respond. Not a minute went by before Titus and Damen reached for their phones at the same time. A sense of foreboding began to grow within me as I watched the two of them, embarrassed.

Surely, Julian did not—

"How could you not have had sweet and sour chicken before?" Titus glanced over his phone at me, his tone incredulous. "That's a *staple*."

"That is not a staple." Damen lowered his glasses and appeared to be deep in thought. "The pork dish is more popular than the chicken. As well as the ma po tofu."

"Nobody wants to eat tofu." Titus narrowed his eyes at Damen, as if the suggestion offended him on a personal level. "Besides, Bianca ate meat at lunch. You don't need to suggest that crap."

"Julian likes tofu," Damen pointed out. "And so do a lot of other people. Vegans, vegetarians…or even those who eat it because it tastes good."

"It doesn't ever taste good," Titus grumbled, turning toward me. I wasn't sure what to expect from him as he held one of my hands in his own larger one and gave me a very serious look. "Don't be like Julian. Please eat meat."

My brow raised as I processed his very strange request. "Julian is a vegan?"

I was surprised. Not anything against vegans in particular, only that I had never met one before. This was fascinating. I wondered if they were like the rest of us.

"Vegetarian," Damen corrected. "Julian would be a terrible vegan—he has an extreme fondness of cheese." He continued to watch Titus over his glasses. "And she can be whatever she wants to be." Then he frowned, considering, before adding to his previous statement. "Except a brain-eating cannibal. That would be very bad. We would be forced to report you to some kind of authority in that case; we would have a moral obligation." His mouth quirked. "Sorry, baby girl, but a line has to be drawn somewhere. Don't worry, the same rules apply to all of us."

I couldn't hold back my laughter at the absurdity, but I covered my mouth in an attempt to stifle it. Damen and Titus, who seemed about ready to argue, froze and stared at me. Their faces twin expressions of something unfamiliar, and the heat rose in my face.

Slowly, both of them blinked simultaneously and glanced at each other. I wasn't certain what kind of eye-speech was going on, but apparently, they reached some sort of mutual agreement. Titus crossed his arms and glanced to the side, and Damen pulled out his phone again.

He spoke out loud, for my benefit. "I'll tell them to get all of the popular dishes, *including* the sweet and sour chicken."

"And enough tofu for one person." Titus sighed, defeated. "I can't go through that again."

"No one is going to make you eat it this time," Damen consoled, but Titus only groaned in response.

Origins

Chapter Twenty

Reprise

"What do you think?" Miles asked, elbowing me. "Isn't the beef and broccoli better than the sweet and sour chicken?"

Titus, who had been sitting at my other side, leaned forward and frowned at Miles. "Don't influence her!"

"I'm doing nothing more than what you've already done," Miles retorted, grinning. "Besides, this poor child needs exposure to *different* types of foods. Not only the things you like. You have no sense of taste."

Julian and Damen, who sat across from the three of us, ignored the conversation. They elegantly ate their own meals while Miles and Titus bickered.

I had a feeling that this type of interaction might be a frequent occurrence.

I was stuffed. And we had so many leftovers. The amount of food they bought seemed excessive, but who was I to judge?

It did bring up one question in particular—why we were eating in the dining room instead of near the monitors? I thought we were supposed to be actively working on a case. Sure, there was *me*, but weren't we supposed to be watching the screens every second?

When I brought up my concerns, Damen waved me off with the assurance that it was under control. It made no sense at all, so I wasn't convinced.

Nevertheless, I was thankful for the break. We had only been working for a short while, but my eyes already were strained.

I had expected to see something—anything—show up. But there had been no indication of any kind of paranormal activity. And that was frustrating.

Ever since I first arrived at this house, there had been a steady stream of activity. Yet nothing new had happened since Damen's spiritual battle. The place was still haunted, I could feel the telltale signs in the air. But outside of that *knowing*, there was only silence.

"Hey." Damen pushed my foot with his, and I raised an eyebrow at him. He grinned. "Since we're having a slumber party, what do you want to do first?"

Titus, who had been drinking from a water bottle, choked and began to cough profusely.

"Titus!" I ignored Damen's question—even though it caused my heart to beat excitedly. Titus could possibly die. I reached over and weakly pounded on his back. "Are you all right?"

After a few heaving breaths, he waved off my concern and stared at Damen with watery eyes. "What are you—"

"Haven't you realized this yet? We are having a slumber party," Damen replied, his voice stern. "Like we do every time we get together."

Titus's confused expression morphed into something else. He grinned, turning toward me. "Of course we are! What do you want to do at this slumber party?"

Was this not a regular activity for them? I narrowed my eyes at his glowing face. "Haven't you all ever been to a slumber party before? All teenagers have slumber parties."

Titus nodded slowly. "I'm an old man, though. It's been a while, so I forgot."

"I've never been to one!" Miles replied. "I was out of the country during those years of my life."

The Grimm Cases

Titus scoffed but returned to eating as he watched us. Julian and Damen observed as well.

Interesting. Perhaps there were things that I could teach them after all. And how sad was that?

"All right." I returned to my seat and pushed away my half-eaten plate of food. There was no time to waste. "It's decided then. Time withstanding, we are going to have the best slumber party ever." I glanced around the room—ignoring the bemused expressions they wore—until my gaze landed on Damen's clipboard.

"Can I use that?" I pointed. "I need to make a list."

Damen smiled as he reached toward the object, removed some papers, and handed the clipboard to me without argument. Meanwhile, the others stared at him, shocked, as he responded, "Here you go, baby girl. Knock yourself out."

I hesitated, somewhat alarmed at their weird behavior. Something odd was going on here, and it was beginning to annoy me.

But whatever.

I decided to put that in the back of my mind—I had a mission. I reached for the board and pen and contemplated where to begin...

It was so much easier to visualize things with lists. And considering this was our first slumber party together, I didn't want to forget a thing. I had to stay organized. Especially for poor Miles's sake—he had been deprived of an essential adolescent experience.

And how very strange it was that French teenagers didn't have slumber parties. In any event, I needed to rectify this terrible oversight.

There were some items that wouldn't make the list, of course. Such as manicures. I didn't have any polish with me; and, unless Titus was carrying some, we were out of luck. A shame, but there was always next time.

Then, since this house did not belong to any of us, we couldn't bake cookies. After all, the obligatory flour party and food fight might destroy

187

the kitchen. It would be rude to make such a mess in someone else's home.

Then another thought crossed my mind. We had a job to do here.

I paused, glancing at Damen. "How do we have time for this? Who is going to watch the monitors?"

"Don't worry about it." Damen shrugged. "The cameras are only there for recording. Even so, we have people on it—just in case."

This wasn't the first time he had made such a statement. "What do you mean?"

"What do you want to do at the slumber party?" Damen changed the subject, his gray eyes pointedly looking at the clipboard. "It's all about what you want."

Right…

I was less enthused now, but trudged forward for Miles's sake. After all, he was radiating delight as he read everything over my shoulder. He was probably so excited—I couldn't let him down now.

I wanted to keep it a surprise, but Miles was relentless in trying to peek. Still, I was able to get most of my list completed without him spoiling the fun.

Watch a Movie

Truth or Dare (or Seven Minutes in Heaven)

Braid Hair

Pillow Fight

Old Maid

But it was still a shock when Miles, who had been chewing on a spring roll near my ear, choked and burst into a coughing fit of his own. I was torn between wanting to help him breathe, and protecting my list from the nasty half-digested food spewing out of his mouth. But, eventually, humanity won.

"Miles!" I smacked him on his back, much like I had with Titus earlier, trying to be helpful. But it was no use. Eventually Titus, Julian, and even Damen had to rush to assist. Whatever it was that caused Miles's issues, it must have been terrible.

Finally, after a tense eternity, his breathing evened and the redness receded from his complexion.

Or, he had looked normal until he caught me staring. Instantly, his face turned bright red again, and he was suddenly unable to look in my direction.

"What is wrong with you?" Damen noticed the strange exchange.

I was slightly affronted—I had done nothing wrong! Oh…Damen addressed Miles, not me. Miles didn't answer Damen's question. Instead, he snatched the clipboard from me and thrust it into Damen's hands.

I could only watch in horror as Julian and Titus stood behind Damen, reading over his shoulder.

This was terrible. I had so much more to add to the list. I hated when people went over my incomplete projects.

There was a momentary pause before three sets of eyes slowly rose from the paper and stared at me. The boys' gazes contained a mixture of bewilderment, amusement, and something else that I couldn't quite place. I began to get anxious.

What in the world was their problem?

"What's wrong?" I leaned away from them. Why did it feel like something was wrong? Perhaps monks hated playing cards—it was too similar to gambling, or whatever. Who knew?

Slowly, Damen turned the clipboard around until it was facing me. Then, just as dramatically, he pointed at the neatly printed 'Seven Minutes in Heaven' item.

Okay?

I pursed my lips, studying the paper. Was I missing something? Everything seemed perfectly normal to me. I glanced back up at him. "What's wrong with that? Do you have something against massages?"

Perhaps it was a hereditary aversion. Finn said he hated that part of Seven Minutes in Heaven too. It was the only thing that made sense. I knew the guys weren't against touching, so I had no idea what the problem could be.

Julian face-palmed at my words, and Titus appeared even more confused. But it was Damen—with a raised brow—who finally answered. He seemed slightly alarmed, but mostly amused. "Massages?"

"Right. Massages."

"Bianca?" Daman's lips quirked briefly, but he continued in a smooth voice. "How do you play Seven Minutes in Heaven?"

Surely, he was joking. Damen, in all his sexy glory, had never played the game before either? I found it hard to believe. But with his serious eyes searching mine, I realized he might be, in fact, not joking at all.

So not only were they monks, but they were sheltered too. It was a good thing they had me. By God, who didn't know how to play this game?

"Well," I began, crossing my legs in front of me as I lectured, "this is a more advanced version of Truth or Dare. The point of the game is to build closeness between friends. You start with your normal Truth or Dare rules, but that's where the similarities end. You see, you can only choose truth. If there's a truth you don't want to answer, then the questioner wins a dare.

"The dares have to be done in order, and you can only withhold the truth three times." I held up three fingers to count off the dares. "The first dare, you simply hold hands with the questioner until your next turn. The second time, you have to sit on his or her lap. But, for the last dare, the questioner wins a massage from the loser."

All four boys were staring at me with looks of disbelief.

"What?" This put me on edge, and I lowered my hand slightly—taken aback. "That's why it's called Seven Minutes in Heaven. Because of the massage—it's seven minutes. It even has its own name—a happy ending."

Titus choked. At the same time, Julian opened his mouth to say something, but Miles, rose to his feet, and smacked him on the back of the head.

I was so confused…

Damen pinched the bridge of his nose. "Where did you hear this?"

Was it possible that I was wrong? Surely not.

The thought didn't comfort me. I nervously picked at my shirt while answering. "Finn told me…We used to have slumber parties, and I was trying to find games for us to play. He told me the details. But then when I researched how to give massages, I found out about happy endings. I had questions. He explained it all…"

"You've played this version of Seven Minutes in Heaven with Finn?" Damen asked, his eyes still closed.

"No." My voice was quiet. The way they questioned me put me on edge. I hadn't realized this was such an embarrassing game. "He said it was stupid."

The four of them exchanged wary looks, and I was even more lost. What did he mean? I had no idea there was another version of the game.

"Never mind." Damen sighed. "This is fine. We can play Seven Minutes in Heaven, baby girl. It sounds…interesting."

Titus was staring at his feet, his expression closed, and Julian's face was disapproving as he rubbed his head, glaring at Miles. Miles—on the other hand—seemed to be entirely too happy about something. Julian sighed, not getting any reaction from the other man, and glanced away—defeated.

"I'm sure there is a rational explanation for this. But at least he didn't take advantage of the situation," Damen muttered darkly.

What in the world was he talking about?

This was not acceptable. Their attention snapped to me as I pulled out my bejeweled phone and unlocked the screen.

Titus frowned, and a spark of caution entered his gaze. "What are you doing?"

"Researching," I replied, pulling up the browser and opening a new search. "Something about this isn't adding up here."

"No!" Julian snatched the phone out of my hand. I could only stare at him—my hand still outstretched—in complete shock. "Don't search for it," his voice was strained as he held the phone out of my reach. "We'll play your version of the game. It sounds like innocent fun."

Damen had returned to his seat and was watching me, amused. "How often do you look up things on your phone? Do you have a computer?"

Why did that matter? "I don't have a computer. If I needed one, I used Finn's. And I research things all the time. I like to be informed."

His gaze turned contemplative. "And you've never searched for these games for yourself? Instead, you asked Finn. I find that hard to believe. You seem like a curious person."

Why were they asking me all of these weird questions? Why were they acting so weird?

"Of course I have! The internet says they don't exist. So I figured that it must be only a local thing or something." I stared at him pointedly. "Are you saying that you know more than the internet?"

Damen held his hands up in an unassuming gesture—but his expression was much more severe than it had been a second before. "Absolutely not," he stated, shooting a look at Titus.

Titus appeared more thoughtful than amused now. "Hey, beautiful?" He held out his hand toward me. "Do you mind if I borrowed your old phone for a while?"

My gaze followed the line of his outstretched arm before I met his eyes. He looked too serious. Miles wasn't laughing anymore, and Julian's embarrassment had fled. The light atmosphere in the room had turned into something darker—something no evil spirit had caused.

Alarm bells rang in my head. No, something was *seriously* not adding up here. Suddenly, I wanted nothing to do with the device.

Without question, I dug the phone out of my pajama pocket and dropped it into Titus's hand. "Keep it." I glanced away. I didn't ever want to see it again—even holding it made me feel dirty.

Chapter Twenty-One

Dark

The party had been cancelled, and my mood did not improve the rest of the evening.

I was just emotionally exhausted. Between everything else that had happened—and now whatever this insinuated. I was stupid, pathetic, and depressed. Miles had attempted to cheer me up with poison-free chocolates—making another store run and everything. But that did nothing to lift my spirits.

There was only one thing that I could do—my job.

While Julian cleaned up from dinner, I limped my way back to the living room and settled myself in an office chair. Someone had to watch these screens. Even though Damen said he had "people" on monitor-watching duty, it probably wasn't the same as me being here.

I had been an idiot about a lot of things, apparently. But taking care of the ghosts in this house was my personal responsibility.

Titus claimed the other office chair and tinkered with my phone and his laptop. Eventually, Julian and Miles joined us in the room but remained silent as they typed on their phones. Meanwhile, Damen seated himself in one of the high-backed chairs. He had been quiet for a long time and just watched me—motionless.

It was somewhat unnerving, but I tried to ignore his unrelenting stare. I was becoming numb to his freakish ways. If staring at a blob entertained him, then he could go for it. I couldn't stop him—I wouldn't be the one to cave first.

"Bianca." Damen's voice cut through the tension in the room like a knife.

I hummed in response, not turning my tired eyes away from the screens. I had won at something, at least. Besides, I knew what his nosy butt wanted anyway. He wanted a reaction, but he wouldn't get it. I didn't care about Finn anymore. Not even Damen's scorching gaze would deter me. I had a job, and I couldn't miss an instant.

"Bianca, look at me."

I pressed my lips together painfully. Why couldn't he leave me alone to wallow? He was so meddlesome and stubborn. I didn't need him to get all psychological on me.

I'd show him. I could be more stubborn. I'd already won once, and I'd do it again. I couldn't look at his handsome face at all right now.

"Bianca! Can you look at me, please?" Damen repeated, his voice commanding.

And, for some reason, I couldn't help myself. I looked at him. Our gazes locked, and the intensity of his concerned expression captured me.

No. I didn't want concern, or pity, or anything else. I wanted to catch this ghost and move on with my life. I was used to disappointment, so I would be fine.

But it wasn't over between Finn and me. I would have to confront him. To get my revenge over his betrayal. No matter what Titus found on my phone at this point, I'd no longer be surprised. In fact, I had a feeling that Finn's betrayal ran deeper than I could imagine.

Why Finn would want to control my phone or lie to me—I had no idea. I almost didn't want to know the reason. It wouldn't change how it affected me.

Something sacred had been destroyed.

"What?" I meant to sound annoyed so Damen would back off. There would always be some things that I'd have to deal with on my own. However, my voice sounded pathetic and broken, even to my own ears.

And for some reason, my vision was blurring—imagine that.

Damen cursed and was on his knees in front of me before I could even blink. Then—just as suddenly—he pulled me from my seat and into his arms as he sat cross-legged on the floor.

"It's all right." He breathed the words into my hair. His voice seemed to reverberate through me as he spoke. "We've got you now. We'll take care of everything. You don't need to pretend anymore."

The way he said it—his words sounded like a promise. It touched me more than anything else ever had. I had been torn—toggling back and forth between two sides of myself.

I actually contemplated ending this friendship before it went too far. After everything that happened with Finn…I couldn't handle my heart being ripped out again by someone else. While it was true that being alone terrified me, being hurt felt even worse.

But there were good people out there. There had to be. I had—apparently—never known them before in my life. But that only made it more likely for me to find someone else soon. There must be something good in store for people who'd suffered the most.

I had to believe it.

There was something different about these guys, and I wanted to believe in this connection. Nothing about this relationship was normal. With them, it was as if my anxieties melted away. Fears and feelings that clouded my mind in any other situation were lifted—I felt like I had regained a part of myself. Even with Finn, it had never felt so right.

Opening up was so easy, and so intimidating. But I couldn't stop myself. I gripped at Damen's shirt, not caring if the fabric became wrinkled. He could buy another. And with that, the dam burst.

"Please don't let this be a lie." I felt pitiful—it was difficult to force my pride aside in order to say the words. Every disappointment flashed through my mind: life in foster care, my adoptive parents, Finn…I was truly alone. "I can't do it anymore."

Damen crushed me so tightly that I could scarcely breathe. But breathing didn't matter. I could only relish the comfort and security of his arms while I broke down completely.

I didn't know how long I cried, but the entire time, he whispered things, made promises, and reassurances that made no sense. His warm hands ran comfortingly through my hair and over my back. The fact that—for the first time in my life—there was someone to simply hold me, who genuinely cared, made me cry even harder.

I was a mess. Yet this cathartic release made me feel stronger. I was no longer alone.

Damen didn't leave me—none of them did. The others hovered and made concerned comments. But eventually, they settled and allowed Damen to take the lead. What was important was none of them abandoned me during my ridiculous emotional display.

Was *this* what friendship was supposed to be like? Was this normal? In the past, Finn would have awkwardly petted my shoulder and left me alone to cry. He wasn't the best person in the world when it came to emotions. I wasn't used to this kind of attention.

It seemed an eternity before my tears dissolved into hiccups. My eyes burned, and as I began to wipe them with my fists—belatedly trying to salvage Damen's shirt—a navy handkerchief was thrust into my hands.

I looked at it—confused. Who in the world carried handkerchiefs these days? Then again, I shouldn't have been surprised. These guys also used serving trays and fine china during their weekly club meetings. So, yeah.

But if they were monks, would it make the weekly meetings a religious service?

Julian—the owner of said handkerchief—sat at my feet, beside Damen.

How long he had been there, I had no idea. Titus was there too, arms crossed against the top of his head as he watched me with a scrutinizing expression. My back was warm—Miles sat on Damen's other side.

I had known they were in the room, but not quite so close! Embarrassment flooded my face. They had all literally sat around me while I cried like an idiot. This wasn't friendship, this was...something else.

It was too much, that was what. Insanity.

Something must have shown on my face. As I accepted the cloth, Damen spoke for the first time in a while. His voice was rough, and from my current position, I couldn't see his face at all. "Don't worry, baby girl. We always sit in close-knit groups during our slumber parties. It's all the male bonding. You've just been initiated."

I half-choked out a laugh—now I knew he was trying to make me feel better. "Stop it." I smacked his chest playfully even as I ignored the pang in my chest. He had admitted out loud I was now one of the boys.

Origins

Chapter Twenty-Two

Answers

Becoming a part of their inner group was easier than I'd thought. I suppose the lack of distinction was made easier by my small breasts. But then I remembered—my job. "The screens!"

I attempted to jump up, but Damen's arms remained tight around me. It was Titus who answered, "I've been watching them. But it's really not important."

"What happened with you looking at my phone? Are you done?"

Call it morbid curiosity.

Titus frowned and glanced at Damen, who stiffened slightly behind me. Just as I suspected.

"What did you find?" It would suck, but I needed to understand how badly I had been manipulated throughout my friendship with Finn. "Just tell me."

Damen sighed. "I'd like to know that myself, but..." He ran his hand down my hair, angling my head so I could see his face. "Are you sure that you want to know?"

I pressed my fists against my chest, as if the pressure alone could calm my racing heart. I nodded affirmatively. Why prolong the inevitable?

Titus's face contorted into a grimace—he wasn't happy. "All right." He held up a small square. "This is your SIM card. I've taken it—and your battery—out because there was a tracker set on your phone."

I had expected this; but it didn't stop the blood from rushing out of my head. Nor did it do anything to quell the anger that had begun to rise in place of my grief. "What kind of tracker?"

"A GPS tracker," Titus replied. "Along with other things."

"What kind of other things?" Damen ground out—his muscles tense beneath me.

"He's been monitoring and recording her calls—a copy is forwarded to his account. The same goes for all of her messages." Titus put the card down and crossed his arms. A mask of fury had fallen over the seductiveness of his face.

It was easy to remember he was still seductive, either way. I had known about the calls and texts already. I couldn't believe fury looked so good on this man as well. How was this even possible?

"He also has a custom parental control program built into the browser. It acts differently than other similar programs. I haven't been able to determine everything that's been withheld, information-wise. But there's definitely terms—phrases—that get flagged when you search for them. The system redirects you to a fake information source, limiting the information you can see. In my opinion, Finn probably controls and updates the software on his own computer."

Julian's fists were clenched against his thighs, and his voice was cold as he spoke. "He shouldn't have the skillset needed for that kind of programming. I thought he wanted to be the chief of police, or something along those lines." He glanced at Damen. "How can he know how to do this? He can't be working alone. What's his major now?"

Damen shrugged. "That's what he wanted to do when he was five, yes. I don't know. He did mention something about electricity when we were home on the holidays. He *could* know how to do these things now. I don't pay any attention to him—he wants nothing to do with us. The only reason why he's at this school is because he has no choice."

Julian and Titus seemed surprised at Damen's statement, and I wondered why. I had known about Finn's childhood dream—so at least that hadn't been a lie. It wasn't as if it was important if it changed; people's interests changed all the time…

"He's majoring in electrical engineering," I said.

Julian shot me a critical look, and Titus grew more displeased. "Then he shouldn't have the knowledge on how to program this kind of technology. That is a completely different field. Does he know information technology or web development on the side?"

I could see the pieces falling into place.

"Not that I'm aware of, but who knows now?" I glanced away from Julian and returned my gaze to my fists. Another piece was being pulled out from under me—but it was the only thing that made sense. "My adoptive father would know how to create something like that. He's a senior web security engineer for the Department of Information Technology."

A consoling weight landed on my leg, and I glanced up to meet Julian's eyes. Something fierce swam within their depths, but when he spoke his voice was as calm as ever. "I know your adoptive parents sent you away before, and that was wrong. No matter how misguided their reasons. So we haven't gotten the best impression of them." He paused briefly, then continued as if he couldn't believe he was asking this. "But do you think your father would have created that kind of program for Finn?"

I swallowed hard, the question not a surprise at this point, but difficult nonetheless. Somehow, I knew that by admitting this—out loud and to myself—everything would change.

But I had to be honest anyway. "Yes."

"Can't you sleep?" Titus asked. Even though his voice was low, it rang loud through the silence of the room.

I rolled over on the couch and looked at him. He had been working at the table for a while, and was now turned toward the room—and me. The dim light of the monitors illuminated his face, and I could see that he was looking directly at me.

The others had gone to bed already. The coffee table had been pushed aside, creating a large space on the floor in between the couch and the two armchairs. Julian and Damen lay tucked among the mountain of blankets and pillows in that square-shaped space.

They must have been tired—I already knew Julian had been—because Julian and Damen fell asleep almost right away.

I ignored Titus's question, and my eyes remained at the two men on the floor. "Do you think we should tell them? Should I wake them up?" I whispered, referencing the cuddling between the two men. I didn't think either swung that way, considering their flirtatious behavior. But who knew…

"No." Titus chuckled. "They'd hate it. Don't ruin my fun. This doesn't happen very often, beautiful."

I wasn't sure what he meant by that, but then he slowly got to his feet and walked toward the head of the couch. I turned onto my stomach and pushed my arms under my chest, watching him now. "What are you doing?"

Titus didn't respond, but pulled out his phone instead. It took me a moment to figure out his intentions.

"Titus!" I scolded, still trying not to wake up the others. "The flash will—"

"Shh," he shushed as he held out his phone in front of him. "It won't wake them. Julian and Damen are deep sleepers. This is just too precious to pass up."

No one was that deep of a sleeper, and I was about to tell Titus so, when it happened. My heart jerked as the light from the camera flashed a handful of times throughout the room.

But still—despite what I expected—Julian and Damen remained wrapped up in each other's arms.

"Why did you take pictures?" I asked as Titus sat cross-legged on the floor by my head. He was so close now, and his nearness made it even more difficult for my mind to quiet. "Are they going to be angry?"

"Probably." Titus was grinning at his phone. "But I won't tell if you don't."

Miles, who had been sleeping on one of the chairs, groggily opened his eyes. "Why are you guys talking? We have classes in the morning."

Titus frowned at Miles briefly, whose eyes were already closed. Then he turned his attention to me. "Can't sleep?" he repeated his earlier question.

I still didn't understand. "How did you know I was awake?"

Titus—instead of responding—inclined his head toward the entryway. Then, without another word, he got up and left the room—only pausing to glance back, indicating I should follow. Which I did, after a moment of indecision. It was either that or lie wide awake with a myriad of thoughts swirling around my head.

Titus was standing at the refrigerator, looking inside, when I finally caught up.

"Are you hungry?" He must be—possibly even starving. After all, who raided a refrigerator that was not their own unless they had a serious hunger situation to attend to? He had eaten so much Chinese food, though. I didn't know how it was possible for him to have room for more food.

Titus closed the door, the gallon of milk in his hand, and gave me a strange look.

"I'm not hungry." He put the milk on the kitchen island before turning back to the cabinets. "You can't sleep."

"But how did you…" Titus turned, mug in hand, and shot me a look that had my words trailing off at the end. Add the fact that Titus was shirtless, only wearing white pajama bottoms, was not the reason why I was suddenly hesitant to answer his question. I suppose it didn't matter how he knew. "No," I admitted. "I can't sleep."

He pointed toward one of the barstools before he poured some milk into the cup and put it in the microwave. I obediently sat as I watched him. "What are you doing?"

Titus didn't answer right away. Thirty seconds later, he slid the warm milk toward me. "Drink. It'll help you sleep." The room was only dimly lit—he never even turned the lights on—but his cheeks held a dark tinge to them.

I glanced at the beverage before meeting his gaze. "I'm not a cat."

Confusion crossed his expression before he grinned. "It's not just for cats," he said. "People drink warm milk to help them fall asleep at night."

"Oh." I looked back at the cup and picked it up. "I never knew that."

Titus leaned against the counter toward me, his weight resting on his crossed forearms. "So, why aren't you able to sleep?"

"Everything with Finn," I admitted.

"Talk to me about what's worrying you," Titus said. "Are you thinking about it in general? Or are you worried he'll do something against you in retaliation?" He frowned before I had a chance to respond, and continued—seemingly believing in the latter option. "He won't hurt you again," he grounded out, his voice terse. "If I have to personally make sure of it, I will."

"Oh." Well, that was kind of him. "I—"

"In fact, I might not even have to do it myself. That might be overkill anyway, considering," Titus mumbled, his arms and shoulders tense.

"What should I do?" I interrupted, trying to get him on the right track.

It was the question that had been haunting my thoughts all evening. Now that I knew these things about my parents—my adoptive parents—I didn't know if I could go back to pretending things were the way they had been. Because I had told Julian that, yes, I did believe my father could have written a program for Finn.

The relationship made sense—on some level. I always suspected their interactions were not normal. But I had been desperate to belong, so I reasoned it away. Before Finn, I had no one. I was too backward and afraid to make friends—even after we relocated. I always had fears, even then: What if no one liked me? Were they talking about me? What if they thought I was bad or strange?

But the close interactions between them—my parents and Finn...Ever since that day I was institutionalized, something was different. My mother, who wasn't the most welcoming person in the world, seemed happier to have adopted me. My father, who had been so quiet, would talk to Finn— my new friend—in private man-to-man conversations, even despite his younger age.

Had they been controlling me, even back then? But why?

Titus wasn't right at all; I drank the milk, but I didn't feel the least bit tired. "What should I do now?" I asked again. "If Finn doesn't say anything, and my mother sends me a message tomorrow. How should I act?"

Titus frowned, deep in thought. "Do you think he'll say something to your parents?"

I nodded affirmatively. "Eventually. He doesn't give up. If he has a goal, he is relentless. If he's been lying to me all this time—if they've been doing it too...then I'm scared. What if..." My heart pounded in terror as memories flashed through my mind. "What if everyone tries to have me involuntarily committed, again?"

"We wouldn't let that happen." Titus's unwavering stare was as steadfast as his words. For some reason, he believed in what he said without a doubt. "Damen, Miles, Julian, and I. We know the truth, and—even though he's trying to deny it, for whatever reason—so does Finn. He also knows that you are with us now. There's nowhere in the world that Finn or your parents could take you that the four of us wouldn't be able to intervene."

Nowhere in the *world*. Just what kind of people were these men?

Chapter Twenty-Three

Dependable

"But my parents…" I tried to explain. No matter what kind of influence they had, it didn't matter. "They still have power to make decisions over me. If mental professionals don't think I'm fit to make personal decisions…"

"Then we'll assign you a power of attorney." Titus shrugged, as if creating complex legal documents was no big deal.

"I would if I could." I sighed, barely noticing as Titus reclaimed my mug. "But I don't think it's possible."

"Why not?" Titus asked mildly as he filled my mug with milk again.

"Because she doesn't have any documentation." Miles suddenly joined the conversation, startling me. He was standing at the entrance to the kitchen, leaning against the wall with his arms crossed. I had no idea how long he had been listening. Titus didn't seem as surprised and continued with his previous actions.

Immediately, I felt guilty. Titus had already been awake, but Miles had been trying to sleep. "I'm sorry, I didn't mean to be so loud."

"You weren't loud at all." Miles joined me at the counter with a yawn. "Titus woke me up. Now, even without your original documentation, or knowing your name, there are still ways. First and foremost is getting copies of the information. Thankfully, the school has records, so we know they exist."

"But I already went to the registrar, and they said they can't give me the documents," I reminded him. "They won't even let me look at them, so I can't get my social security number or my birth certificate."

"They'll give out the copies." Miles sounded so sure. "Don't worry about that. Do you know who you'd like to assign as your power of attorney? Nothing is going to happen—only a fool would attempt something with the four of us aware. But if it makes you feel better, we should get our ducks in a row."

"We?" I asked, again marveling at the cryptic statements regarding their importance. Who knew my new friends had such inflated egos? Then again, the mafia did have ties to many places. Perhaps they were planning on using Titus's brawn and Maria's connections.

How did a monk peacefully come to terms with belonging to the mafia anyway?

"Of course." Titus returned with the mug refilled and pushed it in front of me. "Drink."

So pushy. Even so, I gratefully sipped at it. I had never heard of this homeopathic remedy before, but Titus seemed to believe in it strongly.

"Are you trying to drown her in milk?" Miles raised his brow, eyeing the beverage. "She already had one."

"She said she can't sleep," Titus pointed out. "It will help."

Miles rolled his eyes. "It will give her a lactose overload."

"She's not an infant!" Titus pointed at him. "And not everyone in the world is lactose intolerant."

"Are you lactose intolerant?" I picked up on Titus's insinuation and Miles's slightly jealous demeanor. "But you had creamer in your coffee."

"We are getting off topic." Miles shrugged, not answering my question. "Yes, Bianca…*we*." He looked pointedly at me. It was almost painful to focus on his words, because he had a terrible case of bedhead and his wavy hair was in all manner of disarray. But his warm eyes held my own, taking my breath away. "*We* are on your side—we told you this earlier. One of us, or all of us, will act as your power of attorney if you want. Or you can use someone else. I just want you to be able to relax."

But…It was one thing to be friends, but could I really give them legal rights to make decisions for me? Granted, I would still be in charge of myself. But what if I couldn't…

Would my parents have my best interests in mind anymore? Until very recently, I'd have thought so, but I guess I was wrong. Sadly, it was a fact that I trusted these four men more than I trusted anyone else in my life—and we had just met.

That reality sounded so very pathetic in my head, and I almost cried all over again. Outside of them, I really was truly and utterly alone.

"Bianca?" Miles spoke close to my ear.

I blinked, realizing I had been staring into my half-full mug. My vision blurred, but they weren't tears of helplessness. Not anymore.

"Don't cry." Miles stroked my hair once before looping his arm over my shoulder and pulling me toward him. "I'm sorry if I upset you."

"That's not it." My voice was muffled against his chest. I couldn't believe I was telling them this, but they were so easy to talk to. "I don't know why I trust you guys, but I do. We're practically strangers, but I feel as though I've known you forever. This is weird for me. I never trust anyone."

There was no response to my statement. So much that my face began to warm—I must have sounded so stupid. But it was true, and strange. I'd kept parts of me hidden from Finn and my parents. My true thoughts and feelings being one of them. But with these boys, everything had a way of coming out.

Pushing my hands against Miles's chest, I leaned back to look at him. But he watched Titus with a raised eyebrow instead. Somehow, it seemed as though they were having an entire conversation in the midst of the silence. "Does that sound strange?"

Titus broke their eye-contact first, returning his gaze toward me. "No." His voice was pensive, but also wary. "It's not strange at all."

"We feel it too," Miles interjected, his tone pensive too. "But what we're thinking and your thoughts, are two different things. My theory is unlikely, to say the very least."

Titus frowned at him, his eyes glittering as if he dared him to say more. "It's more than unlikely. Impossible is the better term."

"Nothing is impossible," Miles retorted.

Titus was still frowning and waved his hand in the air, dismissing Miles's statement. "We're not getting into this now."

This new turn piqued my curiosity, and I couldn't help myself. My hands were still on Miles, and I glanced between the two of them again. "What are you talking about?"

"Something we shouldn't be talking about." The disapproval had left Titus's expression, and when he looked at me, there was only sympathy in his gaze. His voice softened. "I'm sorry, princess. We'll tell you one day. But it's late, and it's only been two days since we first met. We really can't—"

I put my hand up, cutting off his apology. "It's all right," I said. I was curious to know what they were going on about, but Titus was right. We had only recently met, and it wasn't like I was being completely upfront about my past either.

I didn't know if I'd ever be ready to cross that bridge.

They would be horrified.

"What are we doing tomorrow?" I asked, changing the subject. "She hasn't come out again tonight, and I don't know if she will during the day..." My voice trailed off as Titus and Miles shot me surprised looks. "I'm talking about the ghost." I supplied helpfully since they seemed to need a reminder.

"That's a good point." Miles perked up, releasing me as he turned toward Titus. "We should probably—"

"No." Titus shoulders tightened, and his green eyes darkened as he watched Miles. "You're going to class. The spirit will wait until tomorrow night. We all have things we need to do."

Miles frowned, "But—"

"We could skip one day," I suggested, studying the two of them. There seemed to be some tension about this topic. But to be honest, I kind of felt like crap. I wasn't looking forward to walking all over campus tomorrow either.

"Miles needs to go to his classes." Titus tore his eyes away from Miles. "And you should too. How is your ankle? Will you be able to be on it all day?"

Miles's eyes flickered toward me. There was a suspicious glint in his gaze, and suddenly, I knew.

He played hooky like it was a sport, and he was dying for me to be his excuse. I wouldn't allow it. Surely as I knew that my name was Bianca Brosnan, I couldn't allow this to happen. Titus had already yelled at him once.

I would have to persevere, even though my ankle did hurt and my body ached. I refused to be the weak link. "I'm perfectly fine," I told them, forcing my expression to stay impassive. "Then we'll go about our usual day and plan to meet here again tomorrow night?"

Titus didn't comment on the crestfallen expression on Miles's face, even though his mouth twitched slightly. "Sounds like a plan," he said. "Just make sure to stay out of trouble until tomorrow night."

So, just avoid Finn. Got it.

The Grimm Cases

Continued In:
Book Two: Ghost

The Author

Lyla Oweds is a paranormal romance author who resides in the beautiful Pocono Mountains, Pennsylvania. She grew up near Gettysburg, Pennsylvania and is a native of Baltimore, Maryland, and has a deep appreciation for the paranormal, hauntings, and Edgar Allan Poe. As such, she loves all things fantasy, mystery, crime, and horror.

She is the author of the Paranormal Reverse Harem series The Grimm Cases and related novellas. She is also in the process of publishing Gloria Protean's story, The Red Trilogy. You can find out more about her current and upcoming works at her website, http://lylaoweds.com.

When not reading, writing, or working as a web programmer, Lyla can be found doing adult-y things such as being a single mom to a toddler and a bird. She also frequently enjoys make-up videos, massages, wine, and coffee.

Made in the USA
Monee, IL
04 June 2023

35263470R00132